WICKED
BRIDE
GAMES

CLARISSA WILD

MUSIC PLAYLIST

"The Demon Dance" by Cliff Martinez
"Are We Having A Party" by Cliff Martinez
"Eyes On Fire" by Blue Foundation
"Scream" by Grimes ft. Aristophanes
"Medieval Warfare" by Grimes
"I Am A God" by Kanye West
"Acid Raid" by Lorn
"Technically, Missing" by Trent Reznor & Atticus Ross
"Consummation" by Trent Reznor & Atticus Ross
"Take A Bow" by Muse
"Anne" by Santigold
"Outside The War" by Santigold
"Aleph" by Gesaffelstein
"Sweet Dreams" by Emily Browning
"Desire (Hucci Remix)" by Meg Myers
"Dark Star" by Jaymes Young
"Only Human" by Cold Showers

PROLOGUE

Accompanying Song: "The Demon Dance" by Cliff Martinez

Nine girls.

That's how many are aligned in this room, including me.

Nine girls with perfect hair and nails, their faces hidden under layers of makeup, their bodies dressed like mannequins from a high-end store.

Nine girls inspected and judged like cattle.

Three men.

That's how many are standing in front of us.

Three men with the most beautiful faces wearing the most devious smiles.

Three of us will be theirs.

We all signed a contract, knowing full well what it entailed. For three weeks, they can do with us what they want, whenever they want, and in exchange, we will receive fifty million dollars. *Each*.

We all thought we knew what we wanted.

We were wrong.

These are the Wicked Bride Games.

The ultimate test to see if we're willing, able, and … greedy enough to want the world.

I want nothing more than to win … And I *will* win.

Even if it means committing cold-blooded murder.

Part I
The beginning

1

Accompanying Song: "Anne" by Santigold

Naomi

"I'm sorry, Naomi, but we have to let you go." The lips of the man in front of me curl up into a short-lived smile. I clench my dress and fight the need to dig my nails into my skin. Or his.

"The company can't continue to do business without making cuts, and unfortunately, your position is no longer required, which is why we've come to this conclusion."

"You can't do this," I say through gritted teeth.

"Well … I just told you we are," he scoffs like my retaliation insulted him.

He shifts in his seat, his Adam's apple moving up and down in his throat as he looks at the sheets of paper in front of him instead of at me. Damn fucker can't even look me in the eye as he tells me I'm finished.

"I *need* this job," I reiterate.

He sighs. "We know you do."

We. It sounds like he doesn't feel a thing while he says it. Like he's not a real person behind this façade.

I wonder what it's like to be in his position. To have the power to accept and dismiss on a whim without having to look out for yourself. I wonder if he goes home every night and kisses his wife without feeling remorse. If he sleeps well. If he'll have nightmares of me screaming at him.

"But that's not possible, unfortunately. I'm so very sorry."

No, he's not. He's just saying that so I'll have empathy for his situation. As if he's the victim for having to tell me this horrible news. No.

"If you were sorry, you'd help me get a different job. *With* the company *or* somewhere else."

He leans forward, holding a pen in his hand, which he swivels back and forth maniacally. He clears his throat and frowns. "I'm sorry, but we currently don't provide such benefits. The only thing I can do is provide you with a letter of recommendation for your next employee."

"And that's it?"

"Yes. You'll receive your final check within three days. I can try to speed it up, but I can't promise anything."

I stare at him in disbelief. "There's got to be something …"

"No, sorry. The boss has already decided."

The boss. Good excuse not to take any responsibility for the layoff himself, even though I doubt the company really needs his position either. He only barks at his employees, even when they're doing their job correctly, so he can sit back and watch them sweat. He knows he has the power, and he loves it. I can see it in his eyes.

Sometimes, I wish I had the same power. I'd use it to screw with people like him and make them pay.

His fingers slide some papers my way, but I don't even look at them as I snatch them off the desk. I get up and straighten my skirt, putting up a front. I'm not about to let this fucker notice my dismay. Not if I can help it. I'll keep my dignity with grace.

So without looking at him, I turn around and walk out the door, hoping he breaks that pencil of his and shoves it up his ass.

***

Later that day

Mom grabs my hands and rubs them. "Your hands are so cold, honey. I just drank a cup of coffee, so mine are nice and warm."

I smile, but the smile doesn't stay. "Thanks."

"You look so pale, Naomi. Are you still eating okay?"

"I'm fine, Mom." I clear my throat, trying not to sound upset. "How's Dad?"

"Oh, you know, the usual."

"He's not smoking anymore, right? Tell me you threw them away."

"I did; don't worry," she says. "Besides, he's not going anywhere. He can't even get out of bed anymore, and he's still coughing up his guts."

The way she describes it makes me wince.

"Is he still taking the meds? You know you have to watch him take them."

"Yeah. I hand him the glass of water myself every morning with them."

"Good." I nod. "If he won't put in the effort, then at least you will."

"Oh, honey … I know your dad can be a … complicated man, but he's only trying to be less of a burden."

"When is he going to understand that he'll never be a burden?" I squeeze her hand.

"I don't think he ever will." She briefly chuckles, but it fades away too. "That's just the way he is. Never accepting any help. Always stubborn."

"Even when he's dying …" I mutter.

"What?"

"Oh, nothing," I add, smiling it away.

I don't want to make her feel bad. I just want to know Dad's okay. Even if he isn't. Knowing he's still fighting the cancer at least gives me hope.

"So how is everything going with you? Still working hard?"

The question makes me choke up a little, but I slowly manage to form a reply. "Uh … yeah, it's fine." I don't want to tell her the truth. It would break her already fragile heart.

I pull away and look at the other people in the coffee shop, contemplating what I'm going to do. I can't *not* do it. I just can't. So I reach into my pocket and pull out an envelope. I slide it to her across the table. "This is for you."

With furrowed brows, she grabs the envelope and sneaks a peek inside then immediately flattens it on the table. "Oh, Naomi ..."

"Take it," I say.

"I can't."

"Yes, you can. It's yours."

"You don't have to ..."

"I want to," I say, looking her directly in the eye, so she knows I'm serious.

"But you need it."

"Not as much as you," I say, and that's the truth.

I may be a cold-hearted bitch on the work floor, but I love my fucking parents to death, and I would kill a son of a bitch for them if I had to. Just so I can see them be happy because, god ... they deserve it after raising a girl like me.

"You're my daughter ..." Tears well up in her eyes. "I'm supposed to take care of you."

"And you're my parents. I have to look after you too. Just let me do this. I can do without it. You need it more than I do."

She leans forward across the table and pulls me in for a hug. "Oh, Naomi ... What did we do to deserve a daughter like you?"

I smile while petting her back, wondering the exact same thing.

And to think I wasn't even sure whether I should do this, considering the fact that it's the last bit of money I have.

I wouldn't do this for just anyone. Family is my number one priority. Anyone else can go fuck themselves. But I'd kill for family.

And after seeing how grateful she is, I know I did the right thing. Dad needs more medicine to cope with his illness. It was the only choice I could make.

"Thank you," she whispers.

"Don't," I whisper back. "Just take care of Dad, okay?"

Her warm hand touching my back gives me hope, even if only for a little while, as she says, "I will."

***

Minutes later

I make my way home in my shoddy old car, trying to keep it from falling apart by braking and accelerating with ease, so it doesn't jam. I wish it would've lasted longer, but I guess that happens when you buy a third-hand car. It's not like I had any other choice, though.

And now, I probably won't even be able to fill her up with gas either.

Sighing, I park my car and get out, slamming the door as I walk to the apartment block. It smells of gasoline and burned food, which makes me pull my nose up as I enter the building. I pass a few doors while breathing through my mouth because the stench from their drugs permeates out their door and through the hallway. As if that wasn't bad enough, the girl upstairs almost always has her door open, ready for men to drop by whenever, and I have no choice but to walk past her home because the elevator is broken. I just look the other way as she's hung up on a guy, her whole room smelling like booze and sex.

13

I try not to think about it as I go up to my apartment, but when I close my own door, I sink to my knees.

God, how am I supposed to last here one more day?

In this filthy building? In this dirty neighborhood?

I'm nowhere. Fucking nowhere.

My purse drops to the floor, pens and lip-gloss rolling out onto the floor. In a fit of rage, I pick it up and throw it at the wall as hard as I can. I scream and slam my hand on the floor.

"Fuck!"

I could scream all day, but that would only make my neighbors suspicious, and that's the last thing I want right now.

I just want my fucking job. No, screw that; I want a better one. I am worth more than that. More than that fucking asshole sitting in that chair handing me those papers. I will not let anyone treat me like that ever again.

I get up and grab a broom from the kitchen to sweep up all the glass shards from the lip-gloss. Without complaining and without making any noise, I clean it up, grabbing a cloth to rid the carpet of the pink stains. I rub in the water and wipe it off until it's squeaky clean again. Until you can't even see one speck ... not one tiny crack.

The light bulb flickers, but I pay no attention to it. It's been going on like this since forever, and I doubt it'll get any better. If anything, my electricity will probably be shut off soon.

A drop of water falls from the ceiling onto my face. I gently wipe it off and gaze up at the chipped, moldy wood above me. Water is leaking from the pipes above. Again.

I sigh. I wish I could ignore it, but after so many failures, how is that even possible anymore?

My life is crumbling. My home is falling apart. And now, my job is gone too.

I get up and throw the cloth in the sink. Then I open the drawer next to my door and pull out the papers to check them. Because of the recent troubles with Mom and Dad, I'd completely forgotten about this … until now.

One week … That's how much time I have to pay the rent I owe before I am evicted. I already have so much trouble paying them on time. I guess they finally had enough.

How am I supposed to pay the rent?

I'm way behind already. There's no way I can make up for the loss of money without a job.

What now?

I can't go to my parents. They have even less than I do. Besides, they need every penny for Dad's lung cancer medicine. I can't ask that of them. And I just gave them everything I had. There's no way I'm ever going to ask for that back.

Biting my lip, I realize I have only three options.

Getting a loan is a small possibility, since I already have bad credit due to unpaid bills. A new job within a week is also highly unlikely, but it's an option.

Or I could just sell some cocaine like my neighbor does. Or sell my body to any random stranger. I bet that would make some decent cash too.

Balling my fist, I chuck the paper away and let it fall to the floor, rubbing my forehead. God, if only it wasn't so fucking difficult.

Money. That thing that makes the world go round. I

need it. I want it.

But every time I come close to earning my fair share, somebody takes it away. It's not fucking fair.

I walk to my bedroom and close the curtains, undressing in front of the mirror. I hate what I see. Not because I'm not beautiful—because I am—but because of how little I've accomplished. With my twenty-eight years, I should already be somewhere. Be someone. I should be an assistant to the CEO of some technology company or a manager at a bank. Instead, I'm wasting my time doing the shitty work for someone who doesn't even want to keep me around.

Annoyed, I turn around and throw myself on the bed, swearing into the blankets.

But as I crawl up, I realize I can only do one thing.

Push forward. Never give up.

So I lie down on my pillow and close my eyes, promising myself that tomorrow's going to be a good day.

***

Accompanying Song: "Eyes On Fire" by Blue Foundation

MAX

The next day

I take a sip of my espresso and watch the customers fly through the bank. Only when a long-legged girl steps into the lobby do I take notice. Still holding my cup, I watch her stride across the tiles on her blue heels, her hips rocking and her long black hair swaying from side to side.

I lick my lips at the sight of her, wondering who she's here to meet. It can't be me; I don't have an appointment scheduled right now, and I'm on a much-needed break. Still, I can't stop looking at her.

She's wearing a tight, red skirt, and an ironed black top. Golden bracelets dangle from her wrist, which makes me think she's dressing to be seen. I wonder if she's going to meet someone high up. It isn't me, that's for sure. I should know, because I own this freaking bank.

I should find out more, but my body refuses to stand as my gaze fixates on her ass. Something about her captures my attention. Maybe it's her straightforward pace or the cold look in her eyes as she passed through the doors.

From a distance, I watch her stand in line, her hands briefly skittering through her hair, and for a moment, I wish it were my hand she felt. I take another sip of my coffee and wait until it's her turn. The color on her tanned face seems to disappear slowly as she talks with the woman behind the glass, her brows drawing together. She pats her hand on the woman's desk and leans forward. They engage in a heated discussion, which only stops when she turns around and parades off toward the door again.

The closer she comes, the more I can see the determination in her eyes—even though she was just scolded and told off. I watch her walk toward me, my eyes unable to look away. The power she radiates draws me like nothing else. She's magnificent.

Exactly what I'm looking for.

I've been waiting so long for this moment.

This excitement. This feeling of electricity running through my veins.

She's the one.

***

Naomi

When I come home, I throw my purse on the table and rub my forehead, sighing out loud. I don't know what to do at this point because even my own bank won't give me a loan. Of course not since I'm indebted to them too. But I thought if I told them my situation, they might help me out. Guess not.

I grab a bottle of water from the fridge and twist the cap off, chugging it down like there's no tomorrow. After a show like that, I need to cool myself down. My body always heats up when I'm in an argument. It's like it instantly goes into fight or flight mode. And I don't ever flee from a fight if I can prevent it.

God, the humiliation. It was just too much.

The way that woman across the counter looked at me as if I was beneath her … I just wanted to pull her underneath the glass and shove my nails into her eye.

How dare she question my ability to pay back this money? Did she think she was better than I was? No one has the right to make me feel like a lesser human. I'm too fucking proud for that shit.

I put my half-empty bottle down on the table and pull the stack of mail from my purse.

I quickly sift through the envelopes to see if it's anything important, other than the looming bills I still need to pay. Usually, I chuck them all into the drawer and forget about them, but the moment my eyes see a peculiar red envelope, my fingers stop moving.

I throw all mail aside except for this one envelope. Strangely, it's addressed with only my first name, and it does not have a return address. I tear it open and pull out the paper inside. At the bottom of the note, it has a signature and the name "Max" engraved. Below that is his address. I wonder who this guy is and how he knows where I live … but I figure maybe his letter will give me a clue, so I start to read.

Naomi,

I know you are going through some money troubles.
How do I know, you may ask?
Well, I might answer that question … after you've come to see me.
Now, I know this might seem odd. To you, I'm a stranger inviting you to come see me out of the blue, but trust me, it is not.
I have what you need.
Money. Lots and lots of it. And I am willing to give it all to you.
You must have many questions—if I am joking, if this is real, and if so, how much, and what the price is. I could answer all of them, but that would make this very boring, and I don't like to play boring games.
Instead, I'd like to invite you to meet me, and I will tell you all

that you need to know.

The real question you should be asking yourself is this, though ...
How far are you willing to go to get what you want?

If you know the answer to that question, come and see me.

2

Accompanying Song: "The Demon Dance" by Cliff Martinez

Naomi

A few days later

With the envelope firmly tucked into my pocket, I exit my building and walk down the sidewalk, the message inside still echoing through my mind. Who is this man? How does he know me? But more importantly, why is he offering me money and what does he want from me in return?

All these questions and no answers make me shiver. Yet … I'm intrigued. I need to know more, even if it goes against every fiber of my being. This has to be a cruel joke played by someone I know. But then why can't I shake the glimmer of hope from my head?

It's all because of that one word.

Money.

Just that one word inside the note got my full attention.

I didn't even need the rest. Just the thought of getting my hands on it makes me greedy. Willing … to do anything.

Maybe I'm insane. Or maybe I just love my family to death, and I want to help them out as much as I can. Or maybe I'm just addicted to the smell of stacked bills.

Whatever the case, I'm about to find out just how far I'm willing to go down the rabbit hole to chase the money.

As I walk down the street, I pass a man in a dark suit who's talking on his phone, but the moment he sees me, he stops for a second. I turn my head and see him blink. Then he turns and walks again.

Frowning, I try to ignore it, wondering what the hell just happened. I don't know the guy, but it looked like he recognized me.

I cross the street and see a black Chevrolet Equinox parked on the corner, two men sitting inside drinking a cup of coffee and eating donuts. They look up, but all I see are sunglasses instead of eyes. One of them stops drinking and the other picks up something that looks like a notepad and a pen and starts to write something down.

I make a face and pass them, trying to ignore it, but I can't shake the feeling of being creeped out by it.

Suddenly, someone walks into me, and I almost fall to the ground. "Jesus, watch where you're going," I growl. When I look up, I notice something in his ear.

"Sorry," he says, clearing his throat. "Are you okay?"

"Uh … yeah," I say, and I quickly walk past him, hoping he doesn't follow me.

But no matter how far I walk, I keep looking over my

shoulder, wondering if there's a man. A man in a suit. A man in a van. A man with a wire.

My skin crawls as I notice the camera hanging from the top of the Starbucks building, and for a second, I wonder if it's filming me on purpose. But I push the thought away because it's ludicrous; every passerby is filmed for his or her own safety. It's normal.

At least, that's what I tell myself.

Maybe I'm just having an off day.

A day when everyone and everything seems suspicious.

A day when I feel like everyone's out to get me ... or to get that money that I so desperately want.

Greed ... it makes you leery.

I hate it.

I breathe out a quick breath and straighten my jacket then decide to call a cab. Better than walking around feeling followed.

The cab takes me to a sky-high building in the center of the city, not too far away from here. I pay the driver and exit the vehicle, passing through the revolving doors of the skyscraper. The marble floors shimmer so brightly I can see my own reflection in them as I look up and down the immense hallway.

A man to my left steps forward. "Excuse me, miss. Can I help you?"

"Yes, I'm looking for ..." *Well, shit. I only have a first name.*

Biting my lip, I contemplate it for a second. "I'm supposed to meet someone here on the fifteenth floor. A man named Max."

"Fifteenth floor?" He cocks his head and narrows his eyes. "Really now?"

"Yes." I clear my throat and pull out the note from the envelope. I didn't want to do this, but he leaves me no choice. I won't be talked down to. Even though I know this place is for the richest among the people, I won't let anyone tell me I can't be here.

The man skims the words and then smiles. "Oh ... right." He looks up at me. "Come right this way, miss."

He holds out his hand and lets me walk in front of him as we follow the red carpet through the hallway. He stops in front of a gold elevator and presses a button. When the doors open, he says, "After you."

I walk past him and enter the elevator, swallowing as I meet my own reflection. I tilt my head up and peek at my hooded eyelids, swabbing away a tiny speck of misplaced mascara with my pinky. I turn around as the man walks inside and presses two buttons, prompting the doors to close.

The wait feels like an eternity, the shifting velocity and pressure inside the elevator making me slightly queasy. When the bell finally rings and the doors open, I inhale a deep breath.

The man steps out and so do I, only for him to point toward one door. "That way, ma'am."

I look at him, and then at the door, and I take a step. He stays near the elevator, frozen in place as I make my way down the long hallway to the single intimidating door at the end.

Because that's what this is.

A scare tactic.

Making your visitors submit to you before even meeting them with a bucket load of wealth and just a hint of authority. Power. The kind that I crave.

Not one second do I hesitate before knocking on the door.

It's not my style, and I don't surrender to anyone or anything. Not even fear itself.

My hand still hovers over the door, almost ready to knock again, when I hear a voice resonate through the walls, sounding like an echo in the dark.

"Come in."

I twist the doorknob and push open the door, stepping inside.

A man stands behind a desk at the edge of the room; his back is to me, and he's gazing out the glass windows that line the room. All I see is wavy dark brown hair, cut neatly in shape, just like his body. His suit barely holds together from his muscles, and for some reason, I can't stop staring at his tight, round ass.

For a second, there's nothing but silence as we both stand still without flinching, without so much as an exchange of words or a breath taken.

Only one thing is going through my mind right now … Who is this man, and what will he make me do for his money?

***

MAX

I peer down at the people below us, wondering what they're thinking as they stroll through the streets, going about their day as usual. I wonder if, somewhere in the back of their minds, they ever wonder if there's more to this life than what they can see or what they know. If they even realize how much of their life is not really in their control.

A wicked smile forms on my lips as I slide my fingers off the windowpane, a silhouette of my handprint slowly disappearing from the glass as if it was never there. Just like those thoughts.

I turn around slowly so I can get a good look at her from top to bottom. Even though I've seen her before, I can't take my eyes off her. With her tall, lean figure and pronounced, dark eyes hiding behind hooded lids, she's a sight to behold.

Seeing someone like that always fascinates me.

That look on her face ... her fearlessness. It makes me shiver in excitement.

"Hello, Naomi."

"How do you know my name?" she asks, her eyes narrowing.

Of course, she immediately wants to know everything.

My lips curve into a smile; a little voice in my head is tempted to tell her the truth, but the devil inside has taken control, and he wants to play.

I place my hands on my office chair and say, "Sit."

It's not a question.

She cocks her head and slowly crosses her arms. "First, tell me why I'm here."

Such attitude. I love it, but she won't beat me at my own game.

I lick my lips as I gaze directly into her smoldering eyes. "Why are you here? You're the only one who can answer that question. But the question you really should be asking yourself is how badly do you want to hear my offer?"

She sucks on her bottom lip and frowns, but then her legs move in the right direction toward the chair in front of me. I pull my own chair back as she stands behind hers, and we both sit at the same time. Just sitting here, I can almost feel the electricity zing between us, teasing me. Showing me a glimpse of what lies ahead …

She doesn't lean forward nor does she lean back as I entwine my fingers and place them on the desk in front of me. I do this with reason, just like anything else in life; to secure my position as the alpha in this room.

But she doesn't seem remotely fazed by my blatant display of dominance.

In fact, with just her eyes, she's deflecting it completely by looking over my shoulder instead of into my eyes.

What a brazen girl … Exactly my type.

"Money," I murmur, the word like a gentle whisper disappearing into thin air.

However, this one word captures her attention immediately, her eyes honing in on mine like a hawk.

"That's why you're here, isn't it?" I ask, smiling gently, but she still won't give me any emotion. Not even a single flinch. "Because of that note I sent you."

"How did you get my address?" she asks.

I raise a brow. "Is that really what you want to know? Or do you want to know how to get your hands on this limited, one-time-only offer I can make you?"

She tilts her head back. "What if I say I'm not?"

I muffle a laugh. "We both know that's a lie. You wouldn't be here if you weren't."

She repositions herself, casually lounging back in the chair. Resting her elbow on the armrest, she props her chin in her hand. "Do we?"

"I know you can't pay your bills. I know you will lose your apartment. I know your bank won't give you a loan and that your final chance is me."

"How ...?" she mutters.

"The hows are not important, Naomi. It's the whys that matter. Ask the right question."

She looks me dead in the eye as she asks, "Why would you want to give me, a stranger, money?"

I nod slowly, intrigued by her quick thinking. "Exactly."

Her index finger touches her temple, and her skin wrinkles in the most beautiful way as she rubs. "You want to know what I'm willing to do for your money."

"Hmm ..." It makes me feel so good when she says it like that. It's as if she can read my mind. It makes me want to grab her and fuck her pussy right on this very desk. I wonder if she can see that too.

I open a drawer and take out a small box, removing the engraved pen I use only for special occasions such as this. I grab the paper lying in the drawer beneath it and place it on the desk. Not too close but not too far either. I want to see her lean toward it. I want to see her ache for the answer. To know what it is that I want … so I can see all the emotions flood her face.

"You will receive fifty million dollars."

Her eyes flicker with a certain greed I recognize all too well.

"If?"

I slide the paper closer to her. "You sign this."

"What is it?" she asks, still not moving one inch.

I thought the mere tease would be enough for her mind to want to crack this puzzle, but it seems she's a lot more stubborn than I presumed.

"It's a contract. You will receive fifty million dollars at the end of our agreement … if you become mine."

She squints. "Yours? Explain."

The right side of my lips tug into a smile. I can't help it; I love her sassiness. Too bad it won't last.

"Mine … to do with whatever I please."

"Like a sex toy."

"More than that."

"Your girlfriend?" She makes a face, and it amuses me.

"Not just that."

"Then what?" Judging by the tone of her voice, I can tell she's agitated.

"Anything and everything."

Her face only hardens more.

"For fifty million dollars, you want me to be your sex doll?"

My brows draw together. "Sex doll? That sounds so crude."

She sighs and closes her eyes, her hand dropping to her

lap again.

"Fifty million dollars. After three weeks," I add, and I place the pen on the piece of paper in front of her.

Suddenly, she gets up from the chair, her face completely void of any emotion. "You've got the wrong girl."

She turns around and starts to walk away, not even granting me one more look. I know what she thinks. *This is illegal. Who am I to even ask? What am I thinking? Have I lost my mind?* She could sue me or call the cops for even suggesting the idea.

But she knows just as well as I do that no one will believe her.

Besides, we both know she needs this, so it's just a matter of time before she comes knocking on my door.

With a grin on my face and the memory of her perfectly swaying ass as it leaves through my door, I say, "I'll see you tomorrow."

3

Accompanying Song: "Anne" by Santigold

The next day

Drip. Drip. Drip.

I rub my temples, trying to ignore the sound, but it just won't go away.

Drip. Drip. Drip.

I should find another job. I should ask more banks for loans. I should ask for a delay in payments. I should …

I sigh. I should do so many things, yet I already know none of them will work remotely as well as the offer I was given yesterday. But the thought of what it means makes me want to tear my hair out.

Drip. Drip. Drip.

Still, sitting here in my apartment doing nothing drives me insane.

I stare at the note lying on the table in front of me; the words beckon me, calling to me in a devious way. Money. It's all I see. All I need. But am I willing to give myself to a man I don't know? A man I've only met once?

Then again, I doubt it's going to go further than just a fuck here and there. A sex doll to the richest man in town can't be that bad. Or maybe I've just lost my mind. Giving away your body to a man you don't know can be quite risky, to put it mildly. But let's face it—where that man lived or worked proved the amount of money he has, and I bet that isn't even one percent of his wealth. The man reeked of money, and it made me so hungry I could practically eat him for lunch. Not to mention he was hot.

Three weeks of him doing anything he wants with me … is that really such a punishment?

The single lit light above me flickers, just like my resolution. And when it finally goes out, I blow out my final breath before I make up my mind.

My home, my job, my life, my family … it's all falling apart at the seams, and I'm not letting it crumble. Not if I can help it. And damn me for wanting to make it big, but I will not settle for anything less than what he's offering me.

I plant my fist on the table and get up, determined to make this choice, even if it'll drown me.

So be it.

At least, I'll have the money to wipe my tears away.

***

An hour later

My hand hovers over his door, but before I can knock, the already familiar voice booms through the wood. "Come in."

Did he know I was coming? Maybe the man downstairs called him to say I was going up. Or maybe he's just been waiting for me all this time. The thought creates goose bumps on my skin. It's not every day that a man is *that* determined to make me his. Then again, I'm a liar if I said it doesn't spook me a little and turn me on in a way I can't explain.

It's like a game to him, and that intrigues me.

So I twist the doorknob and step inside his office once again.

The smile that greets me as he stands up from his chair makes me shiver in place.

"Hello, Naomi. I'm so glad you decided to return."

Again, that voice that makes me melt. God, I hate it so much … that I love it.

"Hello …"

"Oh …" He steps away from his desk and comes toward me, holding out his hand. "How rude of me. I never introduced myself. Max Marino." Before I know it, he's grabbed my hand and shaken it, his firm grip all that I can focus on as our skin touches for the very first time.

When he releases my hand, I can still feel his warmth tingle underneath my skin. As he walks back to his desk, I quickly wipe my hand on my skirt and follow him.

His fingers briefly skim across the paper lying neatly on the desk in front of the chair where I'm supposed to sit. "You're here to accept my deal," he says promptly, not even a hint of hesitation in his voice.

He cocks his head and peeks at me over his shoulder, his fingers sliding across the desk until he's behind it again and facing me. I stand with my heels planted in the carpet, but when my legs shake, I immediately start walking.

"Yes," I answer, and I sit down on the chair opposite to him.

The smile on his face is devious. Telling. Like a young boy who just won a game of catch-me-if-you-can, even though I guess him to be somewhere near thirty. I'd like to wipe that smirk off his face, and I'm sure I will … *after* I receive that fifty million dollars.

"Good," he muses, placing a pen in front of me. "Read through the contract before you sign."

I cock my head. "What makes you think I'll agree to the terms you've laid out?"

"Because you want this money more than anything, and you'll do whatever I say to get it."

"What if I'd like to negotiate better terms for myself?"

"No. These terms are the only ones I'll take." He crosses his arms. "Take the deal or leave it. There is no in-between."

Fuck him for being such an asshole about it.

Grinding my teeth, I mull it over a bit. "How far does this contract allow you to go?"

"Anything and everywhere. There is no limit."

"Toys? Anal? DP?"

34

He taps his pen on his desk, the left side of his lips briefly perking up. But there's no answer.

"Bodily harm?" I swallow away the lump in my throat. Still, nothing. "Could I die?"

His eyes shut, and he muffles a short laugh. "If you died, there'd be no way for you to collect your fifty million dollars."

"Convenient," I say, leaning back.

He places his hand on the paper. "*This* is not just a contract for you. It's a contract for both of us. And if you read this small line here, it says that I must give you the fifty million dollars at the end of our agreement as promised."

I narrow my eyes. "But that means you get to do anything to my body. You could break my bones or cut me up. You could scar me for life and then still give me the money, and our deal would be valid."

He frowns as I continue.

"You could even kill me after giving me the money."

It takes him a while to formulate an answer. "I suppose that's true ... but where's the fun in that?"

I raise a brow. "I want immunity." I place my hand just below his, staking my claims over the contract. "If I take this deal, I will give you myself for almost an entire month to do with as you please, but ... there will be no permanent changes made to my body, whatsoever, whenever."

He smirks, like he knows that even if he agrees, it would still be a possibility that I'd end up with a debilitation and that I'd still only get my fifty million dollars as a comfort prize. But I'm not finished yet.

"*And* ... if you do not follow this contract, you will give me fifty percent of the shares that you hold over your company … *and* my parents will receive the other fifty percent as well as the total fifty million dollars that was promised to me, should I die. Just as insurance for my wellbeing."

His frown deepens.

"Oh, don't be surprised. Of course, a man with your wealth has a company. Probably something like a bank. Or multiple. The only question is how much of it do you actually own?" Now, it's my turn to smile.

"Enough," he says through gritted teeth.

"Great. Then you'll surely agree it's only fair. Money is your life … so a life for a life."

His lips twitch, and he leans back in his chair, staring at me from a distance. "You want to play hard …"

"I know you want me more than I want you."

"Wrong."

"You chose me for a reason," I muse. "I know you want me to believe I'm just some random girl to you, but I know I'm not. There are a million girls across the globe who'd want this just as badly, but somehow, you picked me. That's not a coincidence." I press my elbows against my boobs as I lean forward, watching his eyes go down the slope of my shirt. "You. Want. Me."

For a while, he just stares. Blatantly stares at my chest. Like he's counting his money's worth. Like he already owns me.

"Fine. Deal." He raises his brows. "My shares of the company I work for in exchange for your life. I'll make the amendment in the contract right away." He turns to face his computer, quickly typing something and printing it out to add another paper to the stack beneath me.

I hold out my hand. "Let's shake on it."

He reluctantly gives me his hand, his grip even firmer than before. After that, I pick up the pen and read the document through completely. It states all the rules, which includes my inability to say no. It also says that my family and close friends will be contacted through my own email, stating that I'm going to be on vacation for a month and won't be bringing a cell phone. Supposedly, I'm going off the radar to take a break.

Below that, it asks for my account name and password. Of course, he wants access to that. They don't want me to send secret messages. I smirk, seeing through all of his little plans.

At the bottom of the document are two names. *Naomi Lee. Property of Marino.* That last line makes my skin crawl.

Still, I sign at the bottom. While I put the final dot on the *i*, I ask, "When does the contract start?"

The wicked smile on his face makes me quiver in place. "Now."

4

Accompanying Song: "Eyes on Fire" by Blue Foundation

MAX

Minutes later ...

As we sit on opposite ends in my limo, I can't take my eyes off her. Her olive skin glistens in the sun as it shines through the window she's looking through. She hasn't looked at me since she slid into the car with me. I wonder if she's upset about my proposal, if she has any regrets ... whether she's preparing for what's to come.

She should.

This isn't just some ordinary deal, but she'll find out soon enough. Then again ... she isn't an ordinary woman either.

I admire her from a distance, but my fingers can't help but reach for her face. I gently slide back a few strands of her black hair and tuck them behind her ear. Her eyes flash as she turns her head, her face still completely blank. I wonder what's going on inside that brain of hers. If it's just as beautiful as her body in that skirt.

I can't wait to peel it all away, layer by layer, until nothing is left.

My hand caresses her cheek gently. She doesn't lean away, even though I expected her to, with her feistiness. Instead, her lips tip up into a smile. How strange … and delightfully pleasant.

"Why are you smiling?" I ask.

"For a man who can do anything to the woman sitting next to him, you sure do pick an awfully sweet gesture," she muses, making me smile too.

"That's because I'm savoring you for as long as I can before—" I cut myself off before I say too much. I don't want to upset her. At least, not while I'm in her vicinity. She'd probably kill me if she knew, which is why I won't say a word until we arrive at our destination.

"Before what?" She frowns.

"Nothing." I pull my hand back and clear my throat. "Ignore what I just said."

Her mouth twitches, but she keeps it shut, thankfully. Although I can definitely see her thoughts just from the scowl on her face. I snort.

"What's so funny?"

"Like I said, nothing," I say, shrugging.

"Well …" She stares at her nails and rubs one of them profusely. "If this is how it's going to be for almost an entire month, then I guess this is going to be easier than I thought."

I raise a brow. "How so?"

She smirks. "Because not talking is boring as fuck."

I laugh. "Miss Lee … if there is anything you *do* need to know is that these weeks are going to be anything but boring." I lean in so close, I can smell her perfume. Roses and a hint of honey. I close my eyes and take a whiff. Then I look up at her with half-mast eyes, barely able to contain myself. I'd rather just bite her in the shoulder for trying to taunt me, but I won't. I'll keep it civil … for now.

"I will entertain you thoroughly," I muse, as I grab her hand and kiss her palm. I can feel her shiver.

Right as I lift my head again, my house appears in the distance.

I point at the window and whisper in her ear, "Look."
She turns her head and places her hand on the window. "Is that your house?" Her voice sounds more like a soft breath.

I slide over to her and smile against her earlobe, the touch of her skin on my lips making me want to nibble "That's where you'll be staying. Do you see the fences surrounding the property? Stay within them, or the contract is nullified."

"Okay …"

"What do you think of the house?"

"Well"—she snorts—"it's a nice prison."

"Oh, don't think of it as a prison. Think of it as a castle where all your darkest fantasies will come to life."

She turns her head toward me, unafraid of the fact that I'm sitting so close, so in her space. "My darkest fantasies … or yours?"

I grin as I slide my finger down her cheek. "We'll leave that up to your imagination."

When the car comes to a stop, I clear my throat and slip back into my seat as my chauffeur exits the vehicle and opens my door and then hers.

I hold out my arm for her to grab, which she does reluctantly. "I suppose you're not into the chivalrous kind."

"Oh, on the contrary. I'm just not into you."

Ouch.

"Are you sure you want to be here?" I ask as I guide her along the gravel path.

"No."

"Then why are you?" I tilt my head to the side.

"Money. Plain and simple." She smiles broadly, but it's a fake smile, and I can see right through it.

"You might want to start working for it then ..."

She shakes her head. "That wasn't outlined in the contract. I'm to be yours. It didn't specify how or what my response to your advances should be."

"Hmm ..." I smile to myself. Clever girl. No matter. Soon, she'll find out just how hard she'll have to work for me.

"Still, I hardly believe you're telling the truth about not being into me," I add as we walk to the front door of the mansion. "I saw you shiver when I touched you, and I know you felt it too."

With just one side-glance and a faint blush on her cheeks, I have all I need to confirm the truth.

***

Naomi

He opens the large, wooden front door and holds it open for me to go in first. His eyes are on me like a hawk as I go inside and marvel at the mansion and its marble floors, large floor-to-ceiling windows and drapes, and the intricate tapestries hanging from the wall.

I saunter around the hallway, peeking into the single bedroom on the left with the beautiful red sheets and some kind of hot tub in the corner. "Is this my room?" I ask.

"No, you'll be staying in that one over there." He points at a room above, up the stairs. "The one you're looking at is my room."

I linger near it for a few more seconds, wondering why I can't stay with him. "I like your room."

"I'm sure you do." From the sound of his voice, I'm guessing the answer is a definite no.

"Can I explore the house? I mean if I'm supposed to stay here for almost an entire month, then I might as well make myself at home, right?" I ask with a flattering smile, but it's only to keep up the charade.

"You can but don't expect to have a lot of free time on your hands." He winks, and it makes me look away in silence. I don't want him to see me blush. I hate it. Hate what his smile does to me. I have to focus on why I'm here.

"C'mon," he says, beckoning me to follow him up the stairs.

I quietly trail behind him as we go up and then into a

hallway to the right. There, he opens a door. "This is your room."

I frown as I walk inside, still keeping my eyes on him, as I don't know what he's planning to do.

"Feel free to check it out. There are dresses in the wardrobe that you can wear, and makeup in the vanity drawers. However, you are expected to be ready within fifteen minutes so we can proceed with your introduction."

"We?" I turn to face him. I hope I didn't hear that right.

"Yes, *we*," he muses. "My brothers and I own you now."

My eyes widen, and the temperature in the room just dropped by about twenty degrees.

"Don't look so surprised," he scoffs.

"Brothers? You never mentioned—"

"It *is* in the contract," he interrupts. "The contract only mentioned my last name, which I share with my two brothers." A wicked smile forms on his face.

I step backward, my hands balling into fists. I can't believe he tricked me. Even after I read the contract twice. How did I not see this coming?

The tone of his voice darkens. "We all own you now."

An uncontrollable fury rages inside me as I feel the need to run. So I do. I rush toward him as he exits and closes the door behind him, but before I can get past, he's already locked it tight.

"You can't do this!" I smack the door with a flat hand.

"Actually, I can. You signed a contract. You belong to us now, and we will use you in ways you can't even imagine." His voice echoes as he walks off, the last audible thing being his footsteps as they move away from me.

I twist the doorknob a few times but no luck. Of course

not.

Fuck.

My head drops against the door as I take in a few sharp breaths, my pulse racing.

How could I be this stupid?

How could I have fallen into this trap so easily?

The contract stipulated so little that I thought it was some sort of giant joke, but it also means that whatever's *not* included *can* happen. I gave my freaking soul to him. Willingly.

I ball my fists and slam the door a final time. Fucking fifty million dollars. It'd better be worth it.

"Um ... hi?"

Who was that?

I hold my breath and turn around.

It's a woman, sitting on a couch at the far end of the room, and she's staring at me.

Along with seven other girls.

Part II
The Games

5

Accompanying Song: "Aleph" by Gesaffelstein

Naomi

Day 1

Eight other girls sit in this very room. Eight girls plus me ... all handpicked for the same wicked scheme.

"Hi! Wanna come say hello?" one of them says. She has a round face and shiny blond hair that makes me squint. When I was young, I used to dream of having hair that color. Now, I wouldn't want to be found dead in a ditch with that kind of hair.

Another woman turns around, her long, auburn hair swaying to the side as she glances at me, and then turns her head right back again. "Oh ... another one."

Me. Another one. But how many more?

One girl turns her head and smiles at me, her pearly whites and ocean-colored eyes immediately standing out among the rest. "Oh, hi there." She waves and smiles briefly.

"C'mon, don't be shy." A black woman with beautiful natural curls beckons me.

I take a step forward, wondering where the hell I've ended up.

In hell, that's right.

Nine girls.

Did we all sign a contract to sell our soul?

An olive-skinned woman opposite of where I'm standing says, "Come sit next to me." She speaks with an accent that sounds like she's from India. She pats the empty space on the couch beside her.

She seems the calmest out of all the women. The most trustworthy. So I walk up to her and sit down right next to her. Everyone's staring at me, and I wonder if they expect me to say something, even though I have nothing to tell them.

They were here before me. I know even less than they do at this point.

The Indian girl sticks out her hand and says, "Asya."

"Naomi," I reply, shaking her hand.

The other girls all introduce themselves too.

The pearly white teeth girl is Britt, a twenty-one-year-old model with a thin body and an oval-shaped face. The black lady with the curls is twenty-five-year-old Latisha, a professional dancer.

Then there's Jordan, the thirty-year-old girl with the auburn hair and an aloof attitude. She seems closed off. Camilla is another thirty-two-year-old black lady in the

47

back—she has a pixie cut with red dye in it, and she says she's an assistant to a CEO of a corporation that makes sanitary products.

A girl sitting in the corner of the couch is Hyun, a twenty-year-old Korean girl who seems quite shy, and from what I can tell, she doesn't know much English. From what she explains to us, she works in a coffee shop cleaning dishes.

Next to her is Lauren, a twenty-nine-year-old redhead intern for a video and entertainment company, where she helps upload content to the internet.

Twenty-seven-year-old Stacey, the shiny blond hair girl, has the most perfectly well-done nails I've ever seen, which is no surprise since she owns a hair salon. Finally, there's Asya, the twenty-four-year-old Indian girl who doesn't say much, other than just her name.

And lastly, there's me, the cutthroat half-American, quarter-Vietnamese, and quarter-Japanese bitch whose mission in life is to make big, fat stacks of cash, and that's it.

An awkward silence falls between us as I sit back and wait for them to tell me what's going to happen, but none of them speak up. Ultimately, I'm forced to start asking questions, even though I'd rather not. Asking questions means you don't know, and nothing is worse than showing you don't know … because it's weakness.

But in this case, I have no choice. I have to know what's going on … so I can beat Max Marino at his own game.

"You all signed a contract?" I ask the ladies.

All of them nod.

I shake my head and sigh.

"I know what you're going through," Lauren says,

patting my back like that's going to help. "We never expected it to be like this."

"So you all know why you're here?" I look up, gazing into each of their eyes, but all I see is despair. Fear. Worry.

"We sold ourselves to them," Britt says. "I thought it was a job. That I could add it to my resume. Boy, was I wrong." She snorts.

"Maybe you should've read the small print," Jordan sneers.

They both make faces at each other until Camilla says, "Stop it, girls. We are not here to fight. I know y'all are upset; I am too, but we just gotta deal with it. We should stick together."

"I agree," Stacey chimes in.

Asya sighs out loud. "I don't understand what's happening." She looks at me. "I only came here minutes before you did."

"Who brought you in? Was it Max?"

"Who?" She narrows her eyes.

"The guy with the dark brown hair ..." I say, but I stop because I can see it doesn't ring a bell.

"She was brought in by Anthony. He's a buff guy with long, curly black hair that was so smooth," Stacey says.

She makes a weird gesture in the air with her hand, almost like she's trying to touch him. "He's the same guy who brought me in," she adds. "I was the second girl." She almost sounds proud of that achievement. "Gave me quite a shock when I saw Jordan sitting there all by herself. I didn't know what to expect."

Jordan rubs her forehead but doesn't respond.

"I came in third," Britt adds. "And I was brought in by

some guy named Devon. He had a lot of tattoos, facial hair, and loops in his ears. And his hair was shaved on the sides." She licks her lips. "I knew I shouldn't have trusted him."

"Did they come on to you?" I ask.

"What?" Asya's eyes widen.

"I mean ... did they try to seduce you into signing the contract?"

"No. It was purely business. I thought I was going to be his hairstylist or something," Stacey says.

"Max did," Jordan adds, and she looks me dead in the eyes. "But I ignored his advances."

"Hmm ... so how many of you were brought in by this Anthony guy?" I ask.

Asya, Stacey, and Camilla all raise their hand.

"And who was brought in by Devon?"

Now Britt, Latisha, and Lauren raise their hands.

That leaves Jordan, Hyun, and me. So I point at them and say, "Max?"

They both nod.

Three girls. Three men.

That's *not* a coincidence.

It tells me something important. It tells me that they handpicked us for their own pleasure. Like dolls ... Their favorites to play with.

"The contract. How long is it for?" I ask, wanting to know if we're all in this together.

"Three weeks."

Exactly as I thought.

"And the offer?" I eye each and every one of them to see if they're lying.

"Fifty million ..." Asya whispers.

"Same," the other girls reply.

I nod in concurrence. "Ladies, I guess we've all been screwed."

"But why? What's the point of all this?" Lauren mutters. "Three men and nine women? What do they wanna do with us?"

"Well, I can think of a thing or two ..." Latisha raises a brow and sniggers. It tells me a whole lot about her.

"Please don't," Jordan says, placing her hand over her mouth. "It's already making me sick just thinking about it."

"What is happening?" Hyun suddenly says in somewhat broken English.

Britt gets up and sits down next to her, grabbing her hand. "Nothing's going to happen to us, okay?"

"Three men and nine women?" Hyun repeats. "For fifty million dollars? It's not worth it."

I frown, trying not to say anything even though I desperately want to. I'm not sure whether I can trust these women. Or if I even should.

We've been put in this room together for a reason, I'm sure of it. And it's not just to get familiar with each other either. Let's just say I have a feeling these eight ladies and I aren't going to be best friends when this over.

"They said we had to get ready for something," I say.

"Yeah, I remember that," Latisha says.

"I think we should put on some nice clothes. Put on some makeup." Stacey shrugs when the ladies look at her. "I mean that's why we're here, right? To make those boys happy."

"Right ..." Camilla says, frowning as she gets up. "Well, then let's get to it. Only one way to find out what they want and it's all happening behind that door."

Exactly what I'm thinking.

Even when there are eight more girls than I anticipated, it still doesn't mean I don't want to get that fifty million dollars. They want me ready? They'll get me ready.

"I don't … want to," Hyun says with a soft voice. "I thought this was another job …"

"You don't have to, honey," Camilla says. "I'm not changing, either. They can take me just the way I am. Take it or leave it." She shrugs and then props herself up on her elbows, watching everyone else like it's no one else's business.

Not that I care what anyone here does.

The moment I walked into this room and saw them, I already knew we were rivals. Otherwise, what would be the point of bringing in nine girls when you only have three men?

So I go to the wardrobes in the back of the room and pull the doors open, shoving aside everything that's not my type until I've found the perfect red dress that seems to fit me to a T. I put it on and go to the mirrors on the opposite end of the room, admiring myself before sitting down at the vanity. I pick up a pencil and touch up my eyeliner where needed, and with a brush and some blush, I add a few strokes to my cheeks. I smell three different perfumes and spray on the spiciest one. By the time I'm done, the girls have only just put on a new dress.

I smile to myself and think about all the ways I could screw them over and take their cut as well.

I know … I'm fucked in the head.

But what would you do when you desperately wanted to

cure your parent's cancer?

Let he who cast the first stone be without sin.

As I watch the girls struggle to get ready, I hear a clicking noise at the far end of the room. The entrance.

The door is unlocked, and a handle is pulled.

"Ladies, are you ready?"

It's a voice I don't recognize, but I'm certain I'll get to know it all too well soon enough.

"Time to come out and play." The last two words make my skin crawl.

The girls seem frozen in time, clutching their dresses and their brushes with their partially done makeup, but I am ready to face this challenge.

I stand up and walk with pride toward the door. I meet a man with hair as black as night and looped rings through his ears, his bearded face darkened only by the grimace on his face.

I cock my head as I confront him, smiling viciously. "You must be Devon."

His smile is peculiar—and equally as disturbing as mine is—as he leans against the doorpost. "Well, well … I don't remember introducing myself to you."

"There's no need," I muse. "I know everything I need to know."

His eyes glimmer with a rage I've seen only rarely in men. The kind that reminds me of savage bulls wanting to impale a human being. I wonder if he can restrain himself while I walk past him, underneath his arms. Apparently, he can.

I walk out of the room and go downstairs. I stop in the hallway once I spot two men standing near the door on the left side. One of them I recognize; the other is new but familiar from the descriptions the girls gave me. A man with long, curly black hair and luscious lips. I imagine him being a handsome womanizer. He reminds me of Antonio Banderas in his younger days.

Too bad these guys don't just *play* bad boys … They embody them.

Without saying a word, I watch them with parted lips as they saunter toward me, neither of them uttering one word. I suppose they're enjoying my supposed surprise at their brotherhood. I'm so good at faking it I even surprise myself. *Gag.*

"Ladies, c'mon," Devon says to the other girls, who come running down the stairs one by one like lost lambs.

"Line up," Devon yells after them as he closes the door and comes downstairs too.

I stand at the center as some girls pause on my left and others on my right. Soon, we're lined up and facing three men who stroll back and forth along the line, spinning on their heels to repeat the same thing over and over again. Their eyes never leave our bodies, and they fail to make eye contact even once.

It's like they're judging cattle.

Pricing the meat.

Ready for slaughter.

I swallow away the small amount of nerves bundled in my throat as I stare straight into Max's eyes.

For a second, I think I spot a faint smile on his face, but then his eyes turn cold.

"Listen up, ladies," Max says. "I know you must be confused, so let me explain what's going to happen."

I can feel the air thicken with angst.

It chokes me, even though it isn't *my* fear I'm feeling. It's the *girls'* fear.

"Each of you signed a contract with one of us. You were picked because you are special. You are beautiful. You are smart. You are perfect. Which is exactly why we want you. Why you now belong to us. And it's why we chose you for this game."

"What game?" Camilla interrupts.

Anthony lifts his finger and places it on his lips, silencing her without saying a single word.

"Our game. To win it, you must compete against each other. You will earn fifty million dollars if you win our game. The rules are simple. Entertain us in whatever way necessary, and you will win."

"How?" I ask bluntly, not giving a shit whether I'm allowed to ask questions.

Max bites his lip. I don't know why I see it, but I do. "By doing everything we desire. Whether it be serving us, massaging us—"

"Or undressing for us," Anthony adds.

Devon grins. "Or being fucked in any orifice."

"What?" Jordan's jaw drops.

"Do you mean …" Stacey mutters.

Asya, who's standing beside me, grabs my hand and squeezes it tight. I want to shake her loose, but I know that's not in my best interest now. It wouldn't look good, and I *will* fucking look good if I have to fight these girls for the same prize.

"Yes, you heard that right," Max muses, his eyes honing in on my face. "Sex. Anything goes. Anywhere. Any time.

Any fucking thing that we want, you will do it."

He takes a step into my direction, one foot ahead of the other as he broadens his shoulders, obviously trying to intimidate me.

"Do you want to get fifty million dollars? Earn it. Follow the rules." I know he's talking to all of the girls, but his eyes are on me. "Do not defy us. Do not deny us pleasure. Fail, and you will be eliminated, the contract nullified. That's all. Any questions?"

Eliminated.

I wonder in what sense.

Stacey raises her hand, and Max signals her to speak. "What are the rules exactly?"

Max's wicked smile somehow finds its way into my devious little heart. "You'll find out soon enough."

6

Accompanying Song: "The Demon Dance" by Cliff Martinez

MAX

Evening

Nine girls and three men at one dinner table. Can you imagine the size of the table?

Exactly.

Luckily, the dining room is large enough. It could even fit twenty more people if needed.

I'm not humble, and I like to brag. I know what I have, and I know I was born into wealth, but that doesn't mean I didn't work my ass off to earn what I have.

Case in point—I managed to persuade three of the most difficult girls sitting in front of us right this very moment to sign away all their rights as a human being in a simple contract. And they all fell for it.

I look at my brothers sitting next to me; Devon's

gloating over the meat that's on his fork and entering his mouth, Anthony's enjoying the wine he's sipping slowly as his eyes wander... just like mine.

I can't stop looking at our victory. Nine girls and all of them are a pleasure to the eye. I wonder if they are as equally pleasurable on the cock.

I look at the girls and watch one of them pierce a pea and bring it to her trembling lips. Hyun. She has such a pure, young face; her hooded eyes like black pools I could drown in. Not as beautiful as Naomi's, though, but close. The moment our eyes meet, the pea drops from her fork.

I smile at her, but it only seems to scare her, and she looks away.

I clear my throat and put down my fork. "No need to be scared," I say. "We won't bite."

Devon laughs and quickly covers it up with his napkin when I glare at him.

"But you could," Naomi says. "If you wanted to."

I look at her and smile, wondering if she'll be as courageous to speak up after one of us has our way with her.

Not that I think fondly of giving her away to my brothers ... even though I know I have to share. She, out of all the girls, has the most potential. Simply because she doesn't seem impressed by any of it. And I can't wait to see her resolve crumble.

"I want to," Devon adds without shame, peering at her in a way that makes me want to ram his fork into his hand.

The girls all stop eating, except Naomi, who's still enjoying her rich tomato soup. I could make it creamier for her. Maybe I will later.

"What do you want with us?" Camilla bravely speaks up.

Anthony grins as he places his wine glass down on the table. "Simple. Pleasure. Commitment."

"What does that mean?" Stacey asks.

Anthony eyes her from the side. "We already told you. Anything and everything we want."

"No limits ..." Latisha mumbles.

"Exactly." Anthony winks at her, making her blush.

"So you want us to be your sex dolls?" Britt repeats like she didn't already get the memo.

"Not just that," Devon says. "There's more to it than just sex. I'd like to have fun too."

"Don't," I say, eyeing Devon from the side. He seems offended that I interrupted him, so I point at the food. "We're eating."

"So?"

"I'd like to keep my appetite. Thank you."

Devon rolls his eyes and grumbles but then continues gobbling down his meat like some savage animal. He's always been like this. Boisterous. I guess that's normal for someone who's only twenty-three. Then again, I was *never* like that. At all.

"Use a fork, will you?" I throw him one.

"Mind your own business," he growls, not even touching the damn thing.

Sometimes, I really want to kill him. Too bad Father wouldn't approve.

"So this house ... it belongs to the three of you?" Naomi asks.

The peculiar question immediately captures my attention. Why would she want to know?

"Yes, actually. We live in it together."

"Pity you couldn't afford your own home."

I throw down my napkin as we have a stare down. Her face remains as emotionless as it was before, with the exception of one thing ... a small, victorious smile.

"If I can afford to buy you, do you think I can't afford my own home? This is a family home. One we cherish. One that has special meaning to us. And a purpose. We choose to live here."

"Really? What purpose?" Jordan asks, swaying her wine glass while looking not even remotely amused.

"The purpose of these three weeks ... is to win one of us," I say.

"Put in a different way," Anthony continues, shifting in his seat. "Three of you will be our brides."

All forks drop, along with jaws all around the table.

Naomi is the only one who manages to hold onto it, although her hand is trembling and she's stopped chewing her food. I guess that little bit of information finally got her attention.

"What?" Camilla shouts. "Did you just say brides? As in 'marriage'?" She makes quotation marks with her fingers.

"Yeah," Devon says, "you heard it right."

"You signed a contract. You gave away your body. Your soul. Your rights," Anthony muses.

"Nuh-uh. No way." She scoots her chair back. "Fuck this shit."

"Going already?" I ask, watching as she gets up from her seat, clearly distressed.

"A contract for three weeks, yes, sex, maybe, but I'm not fucking marrying any of you," she says. "I'm outta here."

As she turns and storms away, I call out, "You do realize this stops you from receiving fifty million dollars?"

She doesn't answer. All she does is throw her middle finger up in the air as she waltzes out the door.

"Well, I guess that's settled then." Anthony picks up his wine glass and takes a casual sip.

"Her, out of all the girls ... hmph," I mutter. "I never figured she'd be the one to leave."

"Who'd you expect then?" Naomi suddenly asks out of the blue.

I narrow my eyes, eyeing her from across the table. I know why she's asking—what she's trying to do—but I'm not letting her into my mind that easily.

"I think you can figure that one out for yourself." I give her a poised smile and pick up my fork again. "Let's continue our dinner, shall we?"

The girls all look at each other. Even though I'm eating my salad, and Anthony is finally finishing his steak, none of the girls are eating. They all look like they're on the verge of throwing their forks and knives at us. Or one another. Who knows. I already enjoy this game we're playing, and we haven't even started yet.

"But why would we want to marry you? If we all get fifty million dollars anyway, what's the point in trying to win any of you over?" Lauren asks boldly.

"Well, there's the added bonus of becoming part of the family, which means you'll also automatically become a partner in our business," I say.

"Aka ... more money," Anthony adds.

For some reason, he always manages to finish my sentences. It's like he can read my mind. Or maybe he just wants to one-up me because I'm two years older than he is. He always hated being the middle child.

"So you're basically buying wives," Lauren says, laughing. "Pathetic."

I squint, my eyes twitching from annoyance. "No need to be rude."

"Right ..." Lauren rolls her eyes. "We're the rude ones."

"Look. You either stay for the money and possibly more or leave without any. Your choice," Devon interjects.

"Let's all get back to eating our dinner. We don't want it to get cold." I smile to defuse the situation.

It's quiet for a while. No one says a word, and it's suspicious. I wonder if it's because of the marriage bomb or because of the added bonus of having our name and part of our company bomb.

"No," Jordan suddenly says, her face rigid but weak, like she's holding it together by a thin thread. "You just told us the most crucial part of this contract, without telling us in advance, and you expect us to just *take it*?"

"Just take it?" I muse, swallowing a bite of my salad.

"This is crazy," Jordan says, gazing at the other girls to garner support. "Right?"

None of them speak up.

A wicked smile forms on my lips as I wonder if this is the craziest she's ever been.

It could get even crazier.

Right.

Now.

I scoot my chair back and get up, waltzing toward Jordan. The girls lean back as I focus my attention on her. I grab her wrists, forcing her to drop her utensils, and I pull her up from her chair.

"He—"

I silence her revolt by pushing her down onto the table and putting her hands behind her back, so she can't move.

"What are you do—"

I shove my hand under her dress, crumpling it up. "Didn't I tell you not to defy us?" I say, and in one go, I yank down her panties.

"No," she mumbles as I hold her down against the table.

"Yes. I. Did." I watch the girls sitting around the table, gulping, staring. I hope they take notice.

"Your body belongs to us now ..." I muse as I slide my finger along her slit. "So let me show you what that means."

"Let g—"

I push her face down onto an empty plate and make her look at the girls. "Look! Look at how you're acting. Let them see how insolent you are."

"I did nothing wrong," she says.

"You signed the contract. Do you want that fifty million dollars or not?" I cup her shaven pussy. It feels so nice in my hand, but all I can focus on is Naomi sitting inches away from me... I imagine it being her pussy.

God, I'm a sick motherfucker.

"Do you?" I repeat, applying pressure to her clit.

After a while, she speaks up with a meek voice. "Yes."

"Then you need to realize this body is *mine* to use however I please." I bring my fingers to my mouth and spit on them, rubbing it up and down her slit. "Now bend over and stay down."

I circle her clit as I hold her hands down on her back,

watching the tears in her eyes slowly fade into oblivion, just like her resolve. Just one single tear manages to escape and fall to the table, but it only adds to my excitement.

She stopped fighting. Admitted defeat.

And I fucking love to conquer and win.

She fists the table sheet as I fondle her pussy for all the girls to see. She turns her head and looks at me with doe-like eyes, but she doesn't open her lips. Not once does she beg me to stop. She knows she had it coming, and she's accepting whatever I have to offer.

All for the sweet, sweet money.

Just as sweet as she is.

But I don't even like sweet.

Hell, I'm only doing this to show the girls who's boss. Particularly Naomi, who's still not shown one single drop of fear or pain at the sight of me touching this girl's pussy. No, the only thing I see in her eyes … is the pang of jealousy.

After a while of toying with her pussy, I notice she's closed her eyes, and for a second, her tongue darts out to wet her lips. Wetness coats my finger, mixing with my saliva. I grin.

Two fingers … thrust straight into her pussy.

"Tell me who owns you now!" I pull out my fingers after she held her breath for too long.

"You do," she says softly.

I pump into her again, as I can't and don't want to stop myself. My cock is twitching from arousal. "Louder!"

"You do!"

"Why?" I growl.

"Because I want that fifty million dollars."

"Exactly. You know what you signed up for. Now, show

me you've got what it takes." I spank her ass, and she squeals out loud.

The horrified looks on the girls' faces only make my cock harder.

God, I live for this. The control. The dirty, raunchy sexual deviance.

This is why we do all of this.

This is worth fifty million dollars.

"How does it feel? Fifty million dollars between your legs?" I thrust even faster, picturing Naomi lying here underneath me, squirming from my fingers. "Do you want it?"

"Yes," she murmurs.

"Then fucking come for me," I say with a rough voice, and even rougher fingers as I fuck her tight pussy.

She gasps and clutches the tablecloth even harder, and I grasp the opportunity to take a fistful of her hair and pull her head up so everyone can see the look of bliss on her face. I continue to fuck her pussy with just two fingers until she explodes.

And explode she does.

All. Over. Me.

It's not just wetness pooling out of her, running down her legs, and dripping all over the floor.

It's not just her loud moan that can be heard from across the hall.

I can feel it … inside her … her pussy clenching around my fingers, begging me for more.

But I'm not going to give it to her yet.

I smile and laugh. "Now, I've turned even the most uptight girl into a sex kitten … all for the money."

I pull my fingers out and bring them to my nose, smelling the sweet aroma of surrender… and take a lick.

"Delicious," I whisper, and I gaze specifically at Naomi, who immediately repositions herself in her chair, scratching the back of her neck. I hope this will incite her enough to play the game just the way I like it.

Jordan remains on the table, lipstick smudges all over her cheeks and the cloth, her face dull, empty. Completely sated. Her unmoving body looks like that of a pretty doll crushed after forced into a position it's not used to.

I broke her already.

Pity.

7

Accompanying Song: "The Demon Dance" by Cliff Martinez

That same night

At night, no one sleeps.

I try to, but the girls who can't stop blabbering about how wrong it was what Max did keep waking me up. How he should never have touched her like that. How he should've just told her the rules from the beginning. How there should have been a warning. How, in the end, she actually seemed to like it.

Wait, no. That last bit was just my observation.

I grab my pillow and shove it against my ears, trying to keep it silent, but their voices are too loud to drown out. I sigh and release my pillow. Staring up at the ceiling, I wonder why they don't just go to sleep. Hell, it's not like they're going to think of something useful now. It's three a.m. in the morning. We need sleep in order to think … and to be beautiful.

Because let's face it, that's what this competition is all about. And it *is* a competition. One where three not-so-lucky girls win the right to marry one of them.

I'm not so sure how I feel about that.

On the one hand, I really, really want that fifty million dollars. I'd do pretty much anything for it, including spreading my legs whenever Max snaps his fingers, even though I despise him.

But marrying him … that means I'm stuck with him forever.

On the other hand, maybe that's not such a bad thing. After all, he's one rich motherfucker, and if he and his brothers can dish out fifty million dollars like it's no big deal, then I'm sure there's plenty more for me to enjoy. If I'm married to one of them, half of that wealth becomes mine.

Mine. All that money.

I could do whatever I wanted.

Buy a five-bedroom mansion, get a boat with an onboard sous chef, go to Paris on a whim just for a shopping spree, and wear designer dresses and Louboutins whenever I wanted to. God, life would be bliss.

Too bad I'd have to share the wealth with him.

Pity.

Then again, if he's as good in bed as he showed tonight with Jordan … then that might not be such a bad deal after all. I like it when a man knows what he wants and takes it. I don't like it when he doesn't do it to me.

I turn around in bed and watch the girls argue, spilling wine everywhere as they pour down and drink up glass after glass, getting wasted on the idea that they're stuck doing the bidding of three men for three weeks.

I don't know what the point in discussing it is. We all saw what happened. We all know the rules now. We can decide for ourselves what we do now. And I already know I'm staying. It was never a matter of if. It's only a matter of money.

Jordan sits in the corner of the couch. Clutching a pillow against her stomach, she's gone to a place of no return, and her eyes look cold and dead. Britt tries to give her a cup of tea, but she doesn't even look at it or Britt.

"Jordan ... you've got to drink something," she says.

Jordan just blinks.

Britt sighs. I can see her frustration, even though I'm all the way across the room in my bed.

"C'mere." She holds out her arms and invites Jordan to hug her, but Jordan's stiff as a board. Instead, Britt leans in and wraps her arms around her from the side, ignoring all the signals Jordan's been giving her.

She doesn't want to be hugged.

She doesn't want to be consoled.

She wants to be left alone ... so her emotions can die a quick death.

I know because I've felt the same way every time I had to beg for a loan.

"Are you okay, honey?" Lauren asks, rubbing Jordan's leg, who flinches at the touch.

"Please don't ..." Jordan mumbles.

I crawl up from underneath my blankets and get up.

"Let her be."

The girls look at me. "Weren't you sleeping?" Lauren asks.

"Can't."

"Sorry. I know we're loud," Latisha says.

"It's okay. I can't sleep anyway with all these thoughts running through my mind." That's a lie, but I gotta keep up the good image. The worst thing I can do right now is be shunned by the girls I'm supposed to compete against. I know we're rivals, but that doesn't mean I have to treat them as enemies.

"I don't understand," Hyun mumbles, holding her cup of tea close to her chest. "Why would he do that?"

"You mean touch her pussy?" I say. Hyun's face turns red. "Don't be embarrassed," I add. "I just call it what it is."

Lauren opens her mouth again. "She never said—"

"She doesn't need to say anything," I interrupt. "He can take what's his, anytime he wants, any way he wants. As stipulated in the contract," I reply as I sit down beside them. "Look. We all signed a contract giving away all our basic human rights. I'd say we should be happy they're still giving us a proper meal to eat and a comfortable bed to sleep in."

"Have you lost your mind?" Lauren says, scowling. "Why should we be happy with having our rights taken away? I'm not a fucking concubine."

"Concubine ... exactly. That's what we're going to be now."

"I don't want to," Asya says.

I look at her and squint. "Then why are you here?"

It takes her a while to answer. She shrugs. "My parents ... they gave me away."

70

"Wow, wow. What? Are you saying they *made* you come here?" Stacey asks.

Asya gazes down at her feet, which is all the info I need.

"I never wanted this. I never thought they'd actually go through with it."

I grab her hand and squeeze. It's the least I could do. I don't have much empathy, but I know how to hold a hand, and I know she needs this right now. Even if I only do it so the other girls don't think I'm a total bitch; when, in fact, I really am just that.

"Me neither," Hyun says. "I want money. I don't want this."

"Well, this is what we have, so we need to deal with it."

"How? How in the world do you deal with this?" Lauren points at Jordan as an example.

"By shutting off your emotions." I smile and then turn my face back to nothingness. "See? Like this. I do it all the time."

"That won't work for me, honey," Latisha jokes. "Not that I'll need it. I'm perfectly fine with being their sex doll."

"Whatever," I say, not really caring about her reasons to stay or go. "The point is everyone can either take it or leave it. That's what they said, and Max has shown they mean business."

"Leave? Could we?" Britt asks.

"You mean you want to leave and cancel the contract?" I cock my head. "Why not? Camilla did it."

"Yeah, but how do you know she actually managed to get out and go back home?" Britt adds. "How do you know she wasn't … you know … killed." That last word is spoken in a whisper.

The other girls' eyes widen, and they all look at each other in panic.

"Calm down. No one's getting killed." *At least, not yet.*

"I'm sure she made it home alive," Latisha says. "I don't think those handsome guys could kill one of us. They just want to have fun, that's all."

Jordan shakes her head at that comment but still doesn't speak up.

"So you think she got home safely?" Britt asks.

"Yeah," Stacey says. "I saw her leave the house. No one stopped her."

"Does that mean we can leave?" Hyun asks, looking at me like I'm the one to give her all the answers.

"You could ... no one's stopping you." I fold my arms. "The question is do you want to?"

She bites her lip and looks down at her pajama pants. Then she softly shakes her head. "I need the money. But I'm scared."

"Don't be. We'll get through this." Stacey grabs her hand. "Together."

I turn around and look at the door, rolling my eyes and wondering how I'm ever going to live through these three weeks with girls like them. *Gag.*

I get up and saunter back to bed.

"Where are you going?" Stacey asks.

"Bed."

"But ..."

"Leave or stay. Your choice. I'm going to sleep. Night."

And with that, I tuck myself under the blankets and close my eyes.

However, this annoying voice in my head doesn't stop

whispering dirty little lies into my ears, telling me about how I should be mad. How I should envy Jordan because she got his fingers up her pussy, and how I wished it'd been me instead.

And I fall asleep with the image of Max fucking me with everyone else looking ... satisfied ... knowing that I'm as fucked up as they come.

***

Accompanying Song: "Outside the War" by Santigold

MAX

Evening

I take a sip of my whiskey on the rocks and stare at the crackling fire in front of me. My chair feels like a damn cage, holding me back from where I'm really supposed to be. This room where my brothers scheme and laugh as they play a game of pool on the green table in the back. Their noise distracts me from my goal.

Getting Naomi to submit as quickly as possible and making her pick me.

My grip on the glass tightens as I bring it to my lips and take another sip. This drink is the only thing that relaxes me when I'm stressed as fuck. I can't help it; when I have to share with my brothers, things always get tense. We always want the same thing. Someone has to lose ... and this time, it isn't going to be me.

"So you've got a favorite yet?" Anthony asks Devon as he shoots a ball into the hole.

It takes Devon a while to answer. "No ... not particularly."

"I do ..." Anthony muses, playing coy.

"Who?" Devon asks.

"That girl ... with the olive skin and dark, thin eyes ..." I can see him smile, and it makes me want to smash his face in with my glass.

"Hyun?" Devon makes a face. "I never pegged her to be your type."

"Nah, the other one ..."

I turn my head around the corner and growl, "Stay away from her."

My brothers both look my way, but only Devon opens his mouth. "What's your problem?"

"Stay. Away. From. Her." I just give them the look. *That* look. The one we've learned to respect from one another. The one that says ... I'm going to kill you if you touch what's mine.

"Who?" Anthony asks with a low voice.

I turn my head toward the flames again, picturing Naomi as they dance and lick the surface of the fireplace. "Naomi."

"Don't you mean Jordan?" Devon's voice sounds annoyed. "You stuck your fingers up her pussy on day one."

"I don't care for any random pussy." I drink the last sip of whiskey from the glass. "You can have her."

"Who says I want her? You've already tainted her," Anthony says.

"There are seven other girls. There must be another one you like," Devon says.

"No. One left," I snort.

"Maybe you shouldn't have told them about being brides then," Anthony scoffs. "Then maybe I would still have the one I liked as well."

"Oh, shut up. They would've found out anyway. And Camilla was bound to leave anyway. Too much of a temper."

"And Naomi doesn't?" Anthony's face turns to a scowl. "She's the worst."

"She's impenetrable ... her mind beautiful." I smile at the thought of witnessing her crumple.

"Fuck this." I can hear Devon throwing down his cue. "Why would you claim Naomi? You haven't even touched her yet."

"Because I say so."

"That's not enough." I hear his footsteps coming toward me. "I want a piece of that ass too."

I jolt up from my seat and throw the glass as hard as I can into the fire, shattering it into a million pieces. Then I turn around and growl, "Don't you fucking lay a hand on her."

"Whoa, whoa, calm down, you two," Anthony says, standing between us.

"What's your problem, man? This is how the games are supposed to be played. We all get a taste of each of the women, and then we decide," Devon spits.

"My problem is you not recognizing that I already staked my claim long ago."

"How?" Devon frowns.

I reach into my chest pocket, pull out a heart-shaped locket attached to a thin wire, and show it to him. "This is why she's mine."

Devon glares at it and then at me, his nostrils flaring.

"Okay, look." Anthony grabs his shoulders. "No one's saying she isn't yours. If you really want her, she's all yours. But … you know this is how Dad wants us to play the game. We *all* get to try out the girls, one by one."

Grinding my teeth, I look him dead in the eye, knowing full well what Father wants. "I know damn well how this game's supposed to be played."

"Then do your part, and we'll do ours. Besides, just because I'm interested and have a favorite doesn't mean I'll actually want her for real. It's just that she's pretty, which you obviously already know. Look, the point is … We've not even started yet, and you're already on edge." He playfully pats my shoulder. "Relax a little. Drink some more whiskey." He pours me a new glass and shoves it into my hand. "This is supposed to be a fun month, not one filled with hate. We're brothers. We're supposed to stick up for each other."

"Exactly," Devon pitches in.

He fills two more glasses and hands one to Devon then holds it up in the air and says, "Let's make a toast. To the Wicked Bride Games."

I reluctantly join the toast, wondering how I'm ever going to survive these three weeks without angering my father … by killing my own brothers.

8

Accompanying Song: "The Demon Dance" by Cliff Martinez

Naomi

Day 3

Eight girls align in the hallway.

Eight girls in beautiful gowns, pretty red lipstick, gorgeous black-lined eyes, and heavy makeup.

It's all for one purpose.

These three men standing before us in black suits, trying to impress us with their wealth. Only one thing impresses me, and that's their resolve to get what they want. It's something we have in common because I'll stop at nothing to be the one girl to win this foul competition.

The guy with the smooth, long black hair and chiseled face, Anthony, paces back and forth before us. "Ladies, today is the first day of the rest of your life."

Gag.

"Today, you'll be tested on your resolve. How low will you go to please us?"

Hyun looks down at her shoes as Anthony walks past her, and I can tell from her shaking body that she's terrified. Asya is the same.

"Prove your willingness. Prove how much you want this money we're offering."

He stops when he reaches me and smiles, after looking up and down my body like I'm for sale.

"On your knees."

All girls sink to their knees, even if it takes them a while.

I'm the last to go.

After Anthony placed his hand on my shoulder and forced me down.

"I said on your knees," he hisses at me.

I narrow my eyes at him but refuse to break eye contact until he does, after which he resumes pacing.

"Now, the first game begins."

Devon and Max step closer, and both of them start unbuckling their belts, slipping it through the holes one by one.

"Today, you will eat our cum."

Hyun instantly shifts her face toward the other girls, tears forming in her eyes.

"You will swallow it all."

Now, Asya struggles not to tumble forward as she braces her hands on the floor.

"After dinner, you will lick up our cum again as dessert." Anthony is still pacing around while his brothers have undone the buttons of their trousers.

"If you refuse to do as we ask, you will not be fed, and you will do something else to please us. If you refuse a second time, you will not get a bed to sleep in. And if you refuse a final time … you will be gone."

Gone. Not leaving. Gone. That word … It means something important.

It means that if one of them keeps saying no … she might not be my rival anymore.

It also means winning has suddenly become a lot easier. All I have to do is say yes to everything they make me do. How hard can that be? Once you've shut off your emotions, nothing's difficult anymore.

"Pick your girl," Anthony tells his brothers, and they both nod.

Devon walks around until he stumbles upon a shivering Hyun. He taps his feet in front of her until she looks up at him and begins to cry.

"Aww, how sweet." Devon brings his index finger to her face and picks up a drop. Bringing his finger to his lips, he sucks it up. "I love the taste of tears in the morning."

"Please …" Hyun begs.

"Please what?" he says as he pulls down his pants and reveals he's gone commando. His dick is already half-hard. "Please give me your cock? Say it," he muses.

"No." She shakes her head and closes her eyes.

Oh, boy.

"No, what?" Devon suddenly grabs her hair and forces her head up, making her squeal in fear.

"No! Don't!" Her words come out in short gasps.

He chucks her aside as if she's garbage, and she falls

headfirst to the ground. Jordan immediately grabs her hand and helps her sit up. Hyun sniffs and scrambles off the floor and runs away into the ladies' room, locking the door behind her.

Meanwhile, Devon's wistful gaze makes me believe he's a complete lunatic, and his words confirm it. "Shame."

"You chased the first one away already," Anthony snorts as he looks down at Latisha. "I'll settle for this chick."

Chick. I hate that word. Like she's some sort of thing instead of a human being.

"No worries. Plenty of other girls to choose from." Devon grins as he positions himself in front of Stacey. "Although I was kind of looking forward to fucking her face since she had the porn-star look."

Two feet pause in front of me. I look up. Max's wicked smile is the only thing that can make me suck in a breath.

"Hello, Naomi …" he mutters, just like did back when we first met in his office.

I just gaze and watch him pull down his zipper slowly, unbuttoning his pants.

"No hello back?" he muses.

I cock my head as he pulls down his pants. He's well-packed. The problem is the fact that I take notice. "Hello, Max. I didn't know I was allowed to speak."

"You are … you're just not allowed to say no to me." His fingers curl around the edge of his boxer shorts and inch down slowly until the base of his dick becomes visible … and then pops out for every girl in the room to stare at in awe.

"So does this mean we can leave?" Lauren asks boldly, and the men momentarily stop what they're doing to glare at her. "Since you've picked a girl and all," she adds, swallowing.

"No," Anthony says bluntly after a few seconds. "You will watch us come inside these girls, so you'll know what's coming for you tonight. Now, pay attention and do as we say. After all, pleasing us means winning."

Devon roughly grabs the front of Stacey's throat and rams his semi-hard cock inside without warning, making her gag.

Max's fingers curl around my chin as he forces me to look up at him. "I'm here."

I blink but don't respond as he brings his big cock closer to my face. "Are you going to show me how much you want me?"

I open my mouth and dip my tongue out to lick the tip of his cock. Surprisingly, it doesn't taste that bad. I take another lick.

"Good girl. Just the way I like it." He bites his lip and caresses my cheek, which feels awkward. Then he starts masturbating, rubbing his dick as my tongue continuously circles his tip.

I glance sideways for a moment only to witness Anthony sliding his dick into Latisha's mouth and then holding her nose to prevent her from breathing. Our eyes meet in a moment of understanding as she too handles it like a pro, while I lick Max's cock from top to bottom.

I feel nothing except the urge to take him all the way … just so I can win.

I could say no to all of this, but I don't want to. I could walk out of here at any moment, but I don't. And do you know why? Because the money is more important to me.

Max's eyes close as he adjusts his dick against my lips, rubbing it up and down in my mouth while still jerking himself off. I try to provide ample pressure and spit to make it easier, and when I feel my own pussy thump to the taste of him, I reach between my thighs and start fondling myself.

Some girls look my way, but I ignore them. I don't care what they think.

My clit wants attention too, and this is the only way I can be in control. Even if he may come in my mouth and make me swallow, my orgasm is my own.

So I flick my nub and circle it with my fingers, making it nice and wet. Then I dive into my panties and thrust up my pussy while taking his cock further into my mouth.

His eyes open, and he looks down at me touching myself, a devious smile forming on his lips.

"Are you touching yourself?" he asks with a soft but low voice.

"Yes," I answer without shame.

"Hmm ..." He pulls back a little and licks his lips.

"Is that a problem?" I stick out the tip of my tongue and circle it around the tip of his cock. It bobs up and down as a response.

"No, keep doing it. I like it." He brings his cock back to my lips and rubs them up against me then pushes inside again, this time a little farther than before.

"I can't watch this ..." Asya suddenly gets up and runs away.

"Hmph, another coward," Devon sneers.

"She'll get her fill later," Anthony muses.

Max just grins like a dirty motherfucker, but his focus remains solely on me.

Stacey's gags and heaves make me peek through the corner of my eye, and I can see the terror on her face as Devon face-fucks her like he's in a hurry. He thrusts so fast she can barely keep up, and her makeup is a mess. Then he smears his dick all over her face, spreading her own saliva until she's covered in goo, only to thrust into the back of her throat again with full fervor.

"Is that what you want?" Max murmurs, grabbing the back of my head and tilting it. "Do you want me to fuck your brains out? Because I can … if you ask nicely. I just thought I'd go easy on you, but if you're not satisfied …"

"I am … very satisfied," I muse, and I show him my fingers which are covered in my own wetness. He bends over, grabs my hand, and sucks on my fingers, moaning as he pulls them out again.

"I can taste your arousal." He grins and adds, "Make yourself come. I want to see your face undone as I come down your throat."

He slides his cock down my throat, which is surprisingly easy. I've never had a man who tasted this good—even his pre-cum, which sticks to my tongue. All it does is make me hornier, and for some reason, I don't find what Devon and Anthony are doing so repulsive anymore.

The way Anthony grabs Latisha's neck and squeezes it until she can't breathe, while his cock his still deep down in her throat, only makes me rub myself harder. That kind of power over a human being … I can almost taste it, feel it in the air, as it electrifies my body.

But then I see Devon slapping his cock against Stacey's face, and it makes me want to bite.

"Lick it faster," Max says, pulling me back to his

domain. "And show me how you please your pussy. I'm keen to learn."

I lift my dress for him to see my wet panties.

Even the girls who aren't being face-fucked look at me as I finger myself.

I know they probably think I'm crazy. Maybe I am. But I'm about to come, and there's no stopping the force that's these three brothers. I just hope I can handle them all ... because I know that sooner or later, they'll come at me all at the same time. I just know it. They're that devious.

Max takes a fistful of my hair and shoves his cock farther inside my throat. "Take it deep, Naomi. I want you to feel how badly I've waited for this moment."

He thrusts in and out of my mouth until his base reaches my nose, and I can smell his skin.

"Fuck," he groans, pulling back again as his dick bobs in my throat. He grabs my face with both hands and forces me to look at him. "When I thrust back into your mouth, you come. Understand?"

After I nod, he slams back in again with full force. At the sound of his loud moan, I come undone. I shiver as my body convulses, my pussy releasing in bliss. An explosion in my mouth follows, along with a long, drawn-out howl from Max. His cum shoots into the back of my mouth, and I can feel it run down my throat. It tastes like the devil's cum—so good, so sinful.

"Swallow. Swallow it all," he growls, as he pinches my nose. I do what he says and then open my mouth to show him I finished it all.

He smiles at me, cupping my chin and letting his finger slide all the way up my cheek, almost like he's caressing me.

Latisha's gurgling makes me look away. Anthony's choking her, and he thrusts into her throat then pinches her nose. "Take it. Take it like a good girl," he growls.

She nods and closes her eyes as his balls tense, and he releases himself down her throat. When he's finished, he wipes his cock all over her face, smearing it with cum, and her tongue dips out to lick him clean.

Stacey gags, and it draws my attention away from them. Devon growls out loud, and I see him grasping her face and fucking her like she's some kind of fuck doll. One moment later, he arches his back, howls, and thrusts into her throat a final time. Her face convulses, and she gags a few more times, closing her eyes to take his cum.

"Fuck, yeah," Devon shouts.

When he yanks his cock out, she drops to the ground, coughing up cum and spitting it on the floor.

Suddenly, he slams his foot on her face and forces her to the floor. "Clean it!"

Her tongue comes out, shaking, just like her, and she starts to lick the floor.

"P-please ...." she stutters.

Devon won't even take his boot off her face until she's cleaned the entire floor. "Fucking lick it all. I don't want to see a drop left."

Her eyes are stained with tears, her face is covered in goo, and her makeup is ruined ... just like her dignity.

But I know, looking up at Max, who's blissfully unaware, that I never lost mine.

I am in control ... I always was.

He. Wants. Me.

I could see it in his eyes, the way he looked at me when

I fondled myself as I licked him. He's not even looked at the other girls once, and when he fingered Jordan, all he could do was glare at me.

I'm the one he wants ... so that means I have all the power.

9

Accompanying Song: "The Demon Dance" by Cliff Martinez

MAX

Evening

During dinner, I can only think of one thing ... Naomi's sweet tongue licking my hard cock.

God, I can still feel her soft, wet mouth wrapped around my hard-on as I slide into her throat again and again until I shoot my load into her. And she took it all with a smile.

A fucking smile.

Fantastic.

She's a tough nut to crack, but that only means she fascinates me more. She and Latisha seem like the only girls in for a kinky night. The others ... well, let's just say they need some time to adjust to their new situation.

Tonight, a lot more tension exists in the dining room as

the girls sit at the table and play with their food without even eating one bite. I guess the white sauce with peppers that's richly poured over their medium-baked steaks reminds them of our cum. They should worry more about their soup, though.

Or maybe it's the fact we forced the two girls who didn't participate in our little game this morning to put on a completely see-through, crystal-embedded dress and become our servers for tonight.

Yes, that's right. Our waitresses are Hyun and Asya, and they are serving us in nothing but a flimsy, see-through sparkling dress.

"Come in," Anthony barks at the girls who are still hiding behind the door.

Devon actually had to drag them out of the room to come down here because they wouldn't leave their room. Now it's locked, and they have nowhere to go but here. It's a pity because I really didn't want them to go through this. I know those girls have it tough. They had a strict upbringing and came from a household with a strong regiment, and here … everything they know is broken apart.

We play with these girls to test them, to seek their limits so we can find the right bride.

The punishment part was my brother's concoction. Devon's, to be specific, and Anthony agreed because he heard from our father that the girls can sometimes revolt, and we don't want that to happen.

No, this system works because it forces them to accept what's coming. If not, they get something that's even worse.

It's the way things work, and how they're supposed to go. That's all I know, and even though I don't agree with these heinous rules, we must enforce them so we remain top-dog position in the house.

I watch with an emotionless face as Hyun enters the room for the first time. Her naked body is so fragile and thin like she could fall over with the slightest push.

She holds a tray in her hands and tries to cover her small chest with it, but I can still see her nipples peek out from underneath. Her pussy is clean-shaven and ripe for the taking. And even though I don't want her … I know my brother does.

Devon.

He keeps staring at her with these eyes … bloodshed, almost. Like a wolf who's found its prey, and he's ready to gorge himself on her.

"C'mere," he calls out. His grip on his fork tightens as she moves closer to the table, trembling. She listens to him, even though she looks mortified. Maybe the punishment will work … even though it's against my personal beliefs.

Still, I can't help but sneak a glance every once in a while. I mean a man can only ignore a beautiful, naked woman for a short time. One's bound to look, and there's no shame in feeling attraction and finding a pretty girl aesthetically pleasing to look at.

Too bad she won't feel that way about herself when she struts around and passes roasted potatoes to all the girls without even daring to look at them.

Her cheeks are as red as I've ever seen, and her legs quake under her as she walks toward us.

"Your p-potatoes … sir." She places one on Devon's plate.

"Finally, you behave," he says with a grin, immediately

chopping into his roasted potato like it's some kind of animal he has to slaughter.

"And well, too," Anthony adds. "Maybe all the girls should learn to talk like that. They'd get into much less trouble then."

Britt drops her fork on her plate and stares at us, the furious look on her face amusing. I wonder if she'll do something. I prepare by holding my knife and fork steadily in both hands. A few seconds pass, and she gazes down at her plate again. The moment is gone.

Everyone relaxes again, and I whisper to Devon, "Stop being such an ass to the girl."

"No. She deserves this for defying us," he sneers.

"Focus your attention on the other girls who still need to get cum instead," Anthony muses. "That's what I do anyway. Keeps me smiling."

"Can I …" Hyun stammers. She clutches her stomach and sets down the tray, her body swaying a little. I grab her wrist to prevent her from falling, but luckily, she catches herself on the table. I may be an asshole, but I don't want her to hurt herself.

"What?" Devon's mouth is half-stuffed with potato.

"I …" Hyun begins, but her growling stomach interrupts her. It's so loud; I'm sure everyone in this room heard it. She flushes even more.

"You're hungry?" Devon's suddenly smiling like an idiot. "You could've eaten … if you'd behaved and stayed like a good girl this morning."

"Devon, do you have to be such an ass?" I say.

"Yes!" He slams his fork into the table so hard that it's embedded into the wood. "Those are the rules. You don't play according to our rules; you don't get fed. You do it again; you don't get a bed. That's how it goes."

"According to Dad," Anthony adds.

I shush him, hoping no one heard.

"Hyun," I say, making her look at me and not Devon because I know she's terrified of him. "After you're done serving, you can eat."

She nods in silence, biting her lip, and then scurries off to grab another plate.

I wish I could give her something sooner, but my brothers would probably kill me on the spot for daring to defy our father's rules.

"Asya, come in," Anthony says as he sees the Indian girl appear in the doorway.

She slowly struts in, her see-through dress not covered by a plate, as she's carrying a pitcher filled with wine. Her curves are magnificent to behold. I wish Naomi would've defied our rules so I'd have an excuse to see her naked sooner.

Oh well, that moment will come quick, no doubt.

As she passes with the pitcher, filling glasses on her way, Anthony smacks her on the ass, making her tip on her toes. When I glare at him, he shrugs and says, "What? She has a nice ass."

"Let's just continue with our plan, shall we?" I reply.

He nods and picks up his wine glass. "A toast … to all the ladies in the room. May you win the right to become our brides."

Most of the girls toast, but none do it with a smile.

We all drink in silence and watch Asya and Hyun scurry away to get more food and drinks. Normally, we'd have waiters to do this job, but tonight, it's their duty.

"I do hope you're enjoying the soup," Devon muses, his tongue dipping out to lick off a single drop of wine left on his lips.

Naomi lifts her head right as she was about to take a sip off her spoon. "Yes. It has a lot of great flavors."

"Hmm ... of course, it does," Devon muses.

Shit.

I can already tell where this is going.

I lean over to put my hand in front of his mouth, but I'm too late.

"It has our cum in it!" he shouts with a laugh at the end.

All the girls sit up, wide-eyed, and drop their cutlery.

I shake my head. I wished he hadn't told them yet. I wanted to keep it a secret until after dinner, but of course, he's too excited to keep his mouth shut. He enjoys seeing the terror in their eyes a little too much, and by telling them now rather than later, it only makes their response more extreme. More ... dangerous.

Which is probably not something he thought of.

Britt coughs and gags, her spoon still filled with a bit of soup, even though half of it splashed onto the table when she dropped it. Lauren shoves her plate off the table.

"Fuck you!" she yells. "I'm not eating that dredge."

"You eat what we serve you ... end of story," Anthony says.

"There are plenty of other things you can eat," Devon says with a wicked grin on his face. "But you won't escape our taste."

Jordan scoots her chair away from the table and looks away, her body almost ready to spring up and run.

Meanwhile, Naomi continues to eat her soup.

"Doesn't it bother you?" Britt asks Naomi.

She just shrugs, which makes me smile like a motherfucker.

Stacey suspiciously stares at her, as if she could change her mind at any moment, even though I know she won't. Naomi's opinion on something isn't swayed that easily. I know firsthand.

"Except …" Devon suddenly continues. "*Our* food doesn't have anything in it, of course. And the girls who already got their fill today have normal food. That's our way of being kind."

"Gee … thanks," Stacey sneers, making a face at him. I can swear I hear her then mumble *asshole*.

"So you're saying we have to eat this, but she doesn't?" Lauren says, pointing at Stacey.

"Excuse me, do you have a problem?" Stacey lifts her brows.

"Yeah, I do." Lauren picks up a bowl of tomato soup and throws it all over the table, making the other girls jump up from their seat. "Fuck this. I'm not fucking eating this."

"Why can't we have hers?" Britt asks while gazing woefully at Naomi's plate, who's still trying to eat her soup in peace.

"Because this is how the game goes. These are the rules." Devon picks up his fork and pricks a piece of meat with the end. "Now eat or starve."

Lauren folds her arms and sits back. "No."

"No?" Anthony cocks his head at her. "Excuse me; do you want to end up like those two?" He points at Asya and Hyun, who are just coming back in again.

"Of course, not …" Lauren sighs.

"Then fucking eat," Devon says. "I'm not saying it again."

"What if she doesn't?" Britt asks sweetly, but she's probably inquiring for herself. Naomi's still watching us all like a hawk without chiming in.

"Then she'll be thrown in the cellar … where bad shit happens. And she doesn't want that, trust me," Devon growls, munching on his meat.

It's silent for a second, while none of the girls makes a move.

Suddenly, Lauren lunges forward. She grabs the carving knife for the meat and throws it at Devon with a loud scream.

I turn my head just in time to see Devon block the knife with his plate, effectively changing its course so it tumbles back onto the table. The meat that was on his plate flops down onto the table, leaving one big mess.

The look on his face changes too … into something I hoped I wouldn't ever have to see again.

He shows his teeth as he visibly grates them and then stands up, both hands on the table. "You…" The way he looks at Lauren makes me believe it's going to be even worse than I thought.

"Don't," Anthony says, grabbing his arm, but Devon shoves him away and stampedes toward her.

"I told you what would happen if you didn't listen to our rules," he yells, and he snatches her by the arm and drags her away from the table.

"No!" Britt screams.

"Let me go!" Lauren growls, trying to fight him off, but

it's no use.

"You deserve what's coming for you now," Devon says, laughing like a maniac.

"Let. Her. Go," Jordan says, slamming her fists on the table.

Anthony lights a cigarette and takes a drag before saying, "It's no use, girl … When Devon's made up his mind, there's no stopping him. He's going to make her pay."

"What are you going to do with her?" Asya screams as she puts the pitcher down on the table and watches as he drags Lauren away.

The grin on Devon's face says it all. "I'm going to hurt her … and it's not going to be nice."

Oh, boy.

This is gonna be ugly.

10

Accompanying Song: "The Demon Dance" by Cliff Martinez

Day 5

At times, I can hear Lauren scream for help.

My skin itches with anxiety, and I hate to feel this way. I feel on edge. Like I'm supposed to do something to help her, but none of us can because we all know they'd throw us in the dungeon in the basement with her. Instead, we're stuck waiting in this room until they call us out to play more games … Until they finally decide to release Lauren. I just wish I could somehow rig the game and win it quickly. That way, I wouldn't have to wait all this time to finally know what happened to Lauren.

None of the girls know. No one's been told.

But all of us hear her cry every now and then …

She sounded so different from when she first came in. So harsh, so full of life. A rebel. Now, I imagine her crumpled up in a corner, weeping and wishing it would all be over.

I can't blame her. Devon seems like the worst of them all. I wouldn't want him to touch me with a ten-foot pole. I've already decided he's not the man I'm going for. If it has to be one of these three, it'll be Max. For sure.

Still, I can't help but wonder why he didn't stop his brother. His decision to pull her away from the group and drag her away seemed rash. Irrational, maybe. Although I would have to agree that getting a knife to the head is kind of an insult … but he had it coming.

I never expected it to be Lauren to pull that trigger, though. Jordan? Maybe, considering what she's experienced so far. But I always thought Lauren would be into the kinky shit. Guess you can never judge a book by its cover.

I sigh and flip another page in the book I'm reading, yawning between because of the lack of sleep I've had since Devon stuck Lauren somewhere painful. I wonder what he's doing to her. And I wonder if they'll ever tell us.

Probably not, but from the way Max was looking at his brother, I could tell he didn't agree with Devon's decision. And I can use that dissonance to my advantage.

"What are you reading?"

I look up from my book only to stare right into Latisha's eyes.

I hold the cover up for her to see.

"Nice … So do you know what happened to Lauren?"

I frown and put my book down on my lap. "Why would

I know more than any of you? We were all in the same room."

"I don't know. Maybe you caught something I didn't." She rolls her eyes. "Ugh, whatever. You don't have to be such a bitch about it."

"I'm just simply stating the facts," I say.

"Yeah, yeah." She waves her hands while she turns and walks like she can't even be bothered.

Not that I care. I pick up my book again and continue to read.

"Why are you even sitting all alone over there?" Stacey suddenly asks.

I look up and see her fiddling with Hyun's hair, trying to make a braid, even though Hyun seems uncomfortable.

"Why not?" I reply, raising a brow.

Why can't they all just get out of my hair?

"Because I like to read in silence," I say.

"Oh, and we're too chatty … Of course." She flicks her fingernails at me. "Whatever."

"Whatever … what?" I put my book down but this time for real. "You know; if you've got a question for me, ask. I have nothing to hide."

She purses her lips and looks me up and down. "At dinner. They forced Asya and Hyun to—"

"Please don't talk about it," Asya interrupts, putting her cup of tea down. "I really don't want to be reminded of that humiliating evening."

"Well …" Stacey continues. "You never once said anything to the men to object it."

"Yeah … Why didn't you say something? We were all pissed … except you," Jordan says.

"I'm sorry. Are you accusing me of something here?" I fold my arms and stand my ground.

"I'm just saying it's a little conspicuous that you were okay with all of that."

"I was not okay with all of that," I say, grinding my teeth. "I just know what the rules are, and I abide by them. That's all."

"Why?" Stacey asks, cocking her head at me like it's her business to know.

I narrow my eyes. "I think the better question is ... why wouldn't you?"

"Because they're crazy, maybe?" Jordan shouts.

"I don't think it's that crazy." Latisha shrugs, but the moment she sees the girls' reaction to her response, she turns around and shakes her head, walking into the bathroom. "Never mind," I hear her mumble.

"See? I'm not the only one who knows how to follow the rules."

"But they're insane, and you know it. It's dangerous," Jordan sneers.

"I've told you before; if you want to leave, go. No one's forcing you to stay."

Stacey pulls a little too hard on the rubber band she put in Hyun's hair because I can see the cringe on Hyun's face. "But that's just it ... How do you know Camilla got home safely?"

"Oh, here we go again ..." I rub my forehead with my index finger and thumb. I so do not have the patience for this.

"Enough about Camilla. She's gone from the house. We need to focus on who's still here. And right now, Lauren's in some kind of dungeon basement being tortured while we sit around here doing our hair and makeup. Don't you think that's depraved?" Jordan says.

"Listen. I'm not here to make friends. I'm here for the money. That money they offered all of us. So unless you're not willing to go all the way for that sweet ass money, I suggest you stop complaining," I sneer.

"I'm not complaining," Jordan says, standing up to face me. "I'm saying you just seem a little too relaxed, considering the circumstances."

"Really? What else am I supposed to do then? Sit around and growl to myself all day long?"

"Girls, girls," Britt jumps up and gets between us before things get out of hand. "Let's not fight, okay? We have it rough enough as it is. We don't need this."

"Obviously," Jordan replies.

I keep my mouth shut but my eyes on her. I'm not walking away until she does.

But then someone knocks on the door.

All eyes pull away except mine. Not until Jordan finally turns her head and looks.

"Naomi. Please come out of the room alone."

It's Max.

I open my mouth but stop myself before I respond.

All the girls look at me.

Without saying a word, I turn around and walk to the door, ignoring the ogling that's going on behind my back.

****

Making as little sound as possible, I open the door and step out of the room, closing it behind me. Max is standing in the hall and turns around to face me when he hears my footsteps.

He smiles softly. "Come with me."

He holds out his hand as if he wants to chaperone me somewhere. I narrow my eyes. "Why?"

He cocks his head. "Because I want time alone with you. Now, c'mon." He beckons me to accept his hand, so I do.

Not because I want to, but because I need to in order to win.

He takes me downstairs to the room I adored when I first came here. Before I knew what depravity would go down in this place. How naïve I was. Just thinking about it makes me shiver.

"Sit down," Max says, and he points at the bed.

I do what he says as he closes the door and locks it. Then he sits down next to me, making an indent in the bed that allows him to lean against my side.

"How are you?" he asks.

"Why do you care?" I look up at him.

He frowns, seemingly upset that I asked. "Why shouldn't I? I like you."

"Right." I roll my eyes.

"Why is that so hard for you to believe?"

"Because you keep eight other girls here for your amusement. Oh wait, it's seven now, isn't it? One ran away because she didn't think this game was appropriate. Maybe she had a point."

"Or maybe you remember that fact because you're glad she's gone? Because it means you'll have a greater chance to win?"

I sigh and turn my head away from him. He will not catch me in a lie. I know he sees right through it, so the only option left is not answering that question at all.

His hand is suddenly on my leg, slithering upward. "Tell me you don't like me."

"I don't," I say with an indifferent voice.

But all he does is burst into laughter.

"You can fool them, but you can't fool me." I suppose by them, he means the other girls.

"It's true," I add, trying to make it more believable.

His laughter stops, and his face turns dark. "No, it's not."

"I hate you," I say.

His fingers curl around my thigh in a possessive manner. "Lie."

"What do you want me to say?"

"The truth. Be brave."

I shrug, trying not to let him get to me, even when he does. "I just want the money that you offered me."

"Uh-huh …" His fingers inch up even further until they're right below my pussy. "But you need to marry me for that. And for me to want to marry you … I have to pick you." He leans in and whispers in my ear, "So you'd better start giving me a reason to want to marry you."

I suck in a breath as his tongue wets my skin, drawing a line from my ear down my neck. I'm trying not to shudder; honestly, I am, but this motherfucker makes it so hard for me to ignore my body's response to his touch.

"Admit you like being touched by me … Maybe I'll pick you if you do," he whispers, pressing a kiss to my neck.

"Fine. I can't deny the physical reaction my body has to your advances." I glance at him sideways. "Happy now?"

His lopsided smile makes me shake my head. How am I supposed to keep resisting his charms when he keeps looking at me like that? Like I'm the only one of the eight girls he really wants to get to know?

"It's a start …" he muses.

"Why are you so intent on me being attracted to you? Is it that important? I mean you have seven other girls waiting in line, dying to get that fifty million—"

"I don't want them," he interrupts, and he reaches for a strand of my hair and tucks it behind my ear. "I want you."

"Then why are they even here?"

"Because my brothers invited them."

"No, you got three in total."

A wicked smile forms on his lips. "So you figured that out …"

Fuck.

I turn away my gaze and close my eyes. *Stupid. Stupid. Stupid.*

"You're smart. I like that."

"Yeah well, you still have two other girls you picked, so why me?"

"They were never a real option. None of them are. How many times do you want me to tell you that I want you? But you do have to work for it. I'm not going to make it easy." He leans back on the bed like he expects me to sit on top of him and kiss him or something.

103

"Well, then why are they even here? Why didn't you just invite me?"

"Because I have to. That's how the rules are."

"Who makes the rules?" I ask.

He frowns, looks away, and sighs. "Someone else."

"Your father." I fill it in for him since he doesn't feel inclined to tell me.

He makes a face. "How do you ... oh ..." It seems like he remembers something.

"I listen ... well." I smile softly.

"You never fail to amaze me," he murmurs.

For a second there, I feel like it could almost make me blush. Almost. "Thanks."

"C'mere."

He beckons me to lie down with him, but I refuse. "No."

"Why not?"

"Because you want me to be all fucking sweet and cuddly with you when I'm not, and I can't. I need to know why the girls need to be terrorized for this game."

He sits up. "You mean what I did to Jordan?" His hand is back on my thigh this time, but even closer to my pussy, up until the point that I can feel him graze my clit.

And fuck, does it feel good.

"I can do the same to you ... but better." His tongue dips out again to lick my earlobe. "You only need to ask."

He plants a kiss on my neck and underneath my ear, his lips finding their way to my lips until they briefly touch.

I stand up to avoid feeling my pussy thump.

He sighs. "You can't keep avoiding me, Naomi ..."

"Your brothers. They dragged Asya and Hyun. They

humiliated them," I say, changing the subject. "And you came in their food."

"That's the rules. Deny our request, and you get worse. That's how it goes. And the cum in the food was also necessary to give all girls equal treatment."

"And you agree with that? You actually want to do that?" I cringe at the thought of eating food laced with their cum. I could stomach his, yes, but not the others.

"No, but it's not up to me."

"It's up to your father then?" I pace around the room while his gaze follows my every move.

"No ... my brothers."

"Why can't you oppose them?"

He gets up now too. "It's not that simple. They have equal rights to all the girls. That's how it's been for ages."

"Ages? Oh ... that's new information," I scoff. It is ... I'm just not sure if I should be shocked or disgusted.

"This is tradition. It's how we've always done things in our family, and our generation is no different. We search for the most qualified, smartest, most beautiful women alive and let them compete."

"You mean ... sign a contract and become your naked servant without rights."

"You're not a servant." He points at the door. "And you can leave at any time."

I cock my head. "You have the key."

"Because I don't *want* you to leave." He holds the key up. "You just have to say the words ... and I'll open the door for you."

I take a deep breath and let things sink in for a moment.

"I won't ... if you tell me what happened to Lauren."

The look on his face darkens, and his lips purse to thin lines. "You don't want to ask that question. Trust me."

I raise a brow and fold my arms. "Yes, I do. If you want me to marry you, at least let me know what I'm getting myself into."

He balls his fists, his stance suddenly far more threatening. "Are you sure? There's no going back."

I nod.

Suddenly, he grabs my hand, thrusts the key into the lock, opens the door, and drags me out. He pulls me along the hallway and down a narrow staircase after which we end up in the cellar.

***

Accompanying song: "Sweet Dreams" by Emily Browning

Screams can be heard … much closer than before.

I shudder at the sound as I come closer and closer, and then we stop right in front of the single door at the end.

"Look through the window," Max growls.

I do what he says.

And he was right.

I am *not* prepared.

Lauren's face, bleeding.

Her body naked in a rack, her ass covered in red belt marks.

And Devon … thrusting into her ass wildly.

"He never asks … he doesn't play nice …" Max whispers in my ear as he slides aside my hair. Goose bumps scatter on my skin as I watch the scene ahead. "He's a monster."

"Why?"

"You know why …"

I turn around to face him, pushing away the tears. "Let her out."

"I can't. This is what Devon wants. What she owes him."

"Her blood? Her cries? Her body fucking marked with his lashes? Her ass used while she's not even awake?"

Max just swallows and stares me dead in the eye. "I know what he does. I've seen it every day... witnessed it firsthand. I can't intervene. If I did—"

"If what?" I snap.

"They'd kill me," he says calmly. Like he's already accepted his fate.

"Then fight them," I yell.

Max covers my mouth with his hand and pushes me aside, away from the door. My nostrils flare as he checks the window and then stares into my eyes again. "Don't. Shout. You *don't* want him to hear you."

"You're all monsters …" I mouth through his fingers.

"I am not a monster," he snarls. "But I can be one if you push hard enough."

"Let me go." I try to push him away, but he's cornered me against the wall.

"No. Not until you promise me you won't tell any of the girls what you just saw."

"Why the hell would I *not* tell them?"

He leans in; his lips close to mine as he lowers his hand from my mouth. "Because … you want to win. And if they find out that Devon and Anthony aren't as nice as they think, they're all going to want *me* instead." He smirks. "And neither of us wants that, now do we?"

He's threatening me—blackmailing me—to keep me quiet.

I make a face and then shove him aside, passing him quickly. "I've had enough of this."

"Wait," he says, walking after me.

I increase my pace … but he does too.

Soon, I'm running back into the hallway with him right on my tail. "Don't you run away from me," he growls.

"Leave me alone," I shout back.

Within seconds, he catches up with me. His arms fold around me, and his hand silences my scream.

"Think you can outrun the truth?" he growls. "You don't get to run away from this."

"You said I could leave anytime I wanted," I mumble through his hand.

He pushes me into his room and slams the door shut, locking it again. "I did … but that offer's off the table now."

"God, how convenient for you."

The top part of his lip rises, and he grinds his teeth. "You want to play this game? All right." He stalks closer. "You have no clue, do you?"

"About what? That you're a lying, manipulative bastard? That you and your brothers like to degrade women and use them as your personal fuck dolls?"

"I am *not* a fucking monster, and I am *not* my fucking brothers!" With a face filled with rage, he towers above me, threatening me not to move.

"Oh … Did I step on your heart? Boohoo."

He grabs my wrists and pulls me to him. "You don't fucking understand what's at stake here, but that's okay. You'll find out sooner or later … if you survive."

"What's that supposed to mean?"

"It means I am your only shot at the money you've always dreamed of … And that you should be a little bit more grateful and willing instead of angry."

"Maybe I'm angry because I saw Lauren tied up and in pain," I spit.

"Maybe you're just upset I showed you what you asked for, and you regret it now." He spins me on my feet and forces my wrists to my back, making my body lean into his. "And I am not having it. You asked for this, and I gave you what you wanted."

"Screw you …"

"Happily," he replies. "You know … you may think I'm just as bad as my brothers, but you're wrong. I'm the best you can get. I'm the only thing you deserve. And you know why? Because we're both made out of stone."

He plants his lips on my shoulder, moving upward along my neck with his tongue dipped out as if he's savoring the taste of my skin.

"I'm not your enemy … but I will be if you make me."

"Everyone here is my enemy. Everyone who stands in the way of me and that cold-hearted cash that screams for me to hold it close."

I can feel him smirk against my skin. "I love the way you think. But … make no mistake… I will fuck you if I want to. Whenever. Wherever. Even in front of the girls if I have to, and I will use any tool in my possession to make you submit."

He places pecks along my jawline and then forces me to turn my head toward him. "And you want to know why?"

He pauses, so I ask, "Why?"

The devilish smile on his face confuses me. It makes me want to slap him ... And then kiss him. And then maybe kill him after. "Because I want you all to myself ..."

His hand reaches for my pussy, and I'm helpless to stop him. Helpless against his advances on my body. Helpless ... in my own arousal of him claiming me.

His hand finds its way to my panties underneath my skirt, and he pulls the lace aside to feel me. "I'll let you in on a little secret. When I fingered Jordan, all I could think about was being inside you."

Not one but two fingers.

Sliding up my pussy.

"I know you were watching me," he whispers, thrusting his fingers into my body. "And you were wet for me then ... as you are now."

He's right.

My thighs clench together, yet my entire body is melting into a puddle just from his touch. His voice. His presence. Everything.

"No." I push away from him with the last bit of strength I have left.

"Yes," he says, grinning. "Stop fighting it."

"This is sick. This whole game is sick. Fucking girls like they're your concubines?"

The vicious, lopsided smile on his face makes me hold my breath. "It's the Wicked Bride Games, honey. Get used to it because it's going to get much, much worse."

11

Naomi

That same night, Lauren's dropped in front of our room.

We noticed the loud thud as her body hit the ground, and when we went to check, we found her lying in front of the door … unconscious.

Her body completely botched up.

Eyes red, face stained with blood.

Jordan and Asya gasped in shock.

Hyun even shed a tear.

Not me, though. I already knew what they'd done to her. Still, it wasn't easy to witness yet again.

I don't know who brought her or why or even how.

But somehow, I knew Max had something to do with it.

We dragged her inside and laid her on a soft mat, which is where she's been resting the entire time.

We've been busy all night trying to keep her from fading. It's morning now, and she's finally waking up with a groan or two.

Latisha brings a bowl of lukewarm water to her and pats down her forehead and cheeks to brush away the blood. I grab a piece of cloth to wrap her scratched arm, so it'll stop bleeding. She groans and squirms a lot, so I place my hand on her chest and keep her down.

"Don't move so much; it'll only hurt more," I say.

"Fuck …" she whispers.

Tears stream down her face.

"Get some cold water. And a straw," I tell Latisha, who nods and turns around.

"How is she?" Stacey asks.

"Not too well … but better than last night." Honestly, I don't know because I'm not a doctor, but I don't want to give her more bad news. Besides, Lauren can hear what I say, and she's been through enough already. I just hope we're doing the right thing.

"Ugh … my head," Lauren moans. "What happened to me?"

"You don't remember? You've taken quite a beating," I say, leaving out the nastier parts.

"No. All I remember is being dragged away from the dinner table. And then that foul dungeon." She coughs. "It smelled awful in there. I think … I think it was me," she adds after a while.

I pat her face with the wet cloth. "It's okay." I smile. "You might have thrown up from the pain."

112

"No, it wasn't that ..."

"Just forget about it. I'm sure it was nothing."

She touches her arm and flinches. "Why does everything hurt so much?"

"They beat you with a belt," Jordan says.

I don't remember telling her. Can she spot the marks that easily?

"What?" Lauren's eyes widen.

"Calm down," I shush her.

"Hyun, help me get her up," I say.

Hyun's standing in the corner, staring at us with tears in her eyes. I don't think she stopped crying once last night.

"I can't ..." She's shaking vigorously, so much so that I just ask Stacey instead. I don't have time for wishy-washiness.

"Grab an arm and we'll lift her up."

Stacey does what I ask and pulls Lauren up, while Britt quickly shoves the couch closer to provide back support. Now, she's finally sitting up.

"Here, drink something." Latisha gives the glass to Lauren.

"Thanks ..." She coughs again and then takes a sip through the straw.

It's quiet for some time, and Lauren drinks and drinks until the glass is empty. Her eyes are blank; she's staring into nothingness like she wants to disappear.

"What did they do to me?" she asks, specifically looking at me.

"I don't ..."

"Yes, you do." She suddenly grabs my collar and pulls me closer. "I can see it in your eyes. The guilt."

Another cough, this time with blood, spatters all over my face, and Britt and Stacey jump in to help Lauren stay upright and pat her down with the cloth.

Meanwhile, I'm just sitting here, baffled, trying to keep my composure.

"Get away from me!" She pushes the girls off her, and they immediately back off.

"You ... you're the reason this happened to me. If they'd given all the girls proper soup, maybe I wouldn't have had to spill mine."

"That's not my—"

"Yes, it is! You could've offered to share," she yells right in my face. "Instead, you did nothing." She directs her attention toward all the girls in the room. "All of you did *nothing* to save me. Nothing!"

"That's not true ..." I whisper. "I pleaded with Max; honestly, I did."

She shakes her head, biting her lip as she fights the tears.

"It's not us you should be mad at. It's them," Stacey says softly.

"Shut up. Just shut up," Lauren cries out then she bursts into tears.

I do the only thing I can and pull her into my arms, holding her close to my beating heart, even though it's cold as stone. At least she'll have a human soul to cling to; unlike those brothers who used her like she wasn't even alive.

I pat her head and let her cry onto my nightgown. I suppose it's the least I can do after not giving her what she wanted during dinner ... after seeing her suffer like that.

Maybe it is my fault, even if only a little.

It still hurts. Because I hate *not* being perfect.

"Did they hit her?" Britt asks softly.

I nod.

"Not just that … I remember … bits and pieces of pain … on my face and in my ass," Lauren mumbles, sniffing.

"Oh, my god …" Britt smacks her hand against her mouth, shaking her head vehemently.

"Please, don't," Hyun whispers. "Please, just … no more."

"This is what happened to Lauren," I say. "You can't deny it."

"I can't handle it," Hyun says in broken English. "I just can't. I don't know why we're still here. I don't want this. Who does? Let's just run. Let's get out of here before it's too late."

"No," I say abruptly.

"Yeah, I get Hyun's point," Jordan says.

"No, you *can't* leave. Not now." I try to point at Lauren, but it's hard when I'm consoling her too.

"We can. If we do it together," Stacey mumbles as she stares into the distance.

"No, you don't understand," I hiss. "They'll. Kill. Her."

I'm trying to prevent Lauren from hearing, but it fails.

"I don't wanna die," she mewls.

"*No one* wants to die," I answer. "And if we run, then Lauren is left to fend for herself. She can't walk. She can barely sit up. We can't carry her."

"Maybe if we used a blanket?" Stacey suggests.

"No. That's ridiculous. It won't work. I don't understand why you're even thinking of this." I sigh. "You want to leave? Fine. Leave. But I'm staying here."

I hug Lauren tight as she wraps her arms around my

body and weeps out her pain.

The other girls just stare with bitter and confused expressions. I'm certain none of them know what to do at this point, and neither do I. But continuing is better than quitting. We've already gotten this far, right?

"Be strong," I whisper in Lauren's ear. "You'll make it through this."

"I'm so fucking angry," she says, and I can feel her muscles tense up against my body. "I just want to scream and hurt someone."

"I know, and you'll get your chance later. Just focus on surviving for now."

"Surviving, for what? To marry one of them?" she yells. "I hate them. I fucking hate them. I could never marry a guy I don't love."

I shush her again and pull her closer so she can't talk anymore. She needs to save her energy for healing. Maybe later, we can get her in the shower and clean her up. But for now, she needs to rest.

"What if we call the police?" Stacey says.

I roll my eyes. "That won't work. They'll never believe us. Max, Devon, and Anthony have them in their pocket; I just know it. I mean just look at their wealth. You don't get that rich without bribing someone."

Stacey nods slowly, frowning in annoyance.

"Besides, they already told our family and friends we were here on vacation, so calling them won't work either."

"It's like they planned it all ahead," Latisha muses.

For a second, I wish she didn't know that tiny fact.

"I can't do this anymore," Hyun suddenly says.

And with those words, she turns around, twists the door

116

handle, and walks out.

I guess sometimes the pressure gets too much, and those who are at the bottom of the food chain give up the fight. Natural selection.

***

Accompanying Song: "Are We Having A Party" by Cliff Martinez

MAX

Day 8

All girls stand in a line in the hall again. All except the two who ran away.

Pity. I'd hoped they'd last a bit longer so they could keep my brothers busy while I focused on Naomi, but I guess these games became a little too much for them.

No matter—plenty of girls still left to enjoy.

Plenty who will eventually crack.

I lick my lips as I look at each of them in their beautiful gold dresses that we asked them to wear. Their thick-lined eyes and overdone makeup won't hide the nervous eye movements. I can spot it from miles away. They're waiting … waiting for us like good little dolls. Despite the fact that bruises still cover Lauren, she's still here, staring blankly into space. Exactly as she should.

Don't give up.

Even if only so my brothers can still pick someone other than Naomi.

Because by god ... that woman is *mine.*

"So ... are all of you ready for your next task?" I ask.

None of them reply. Only Naomi cocks her head—like she's curious, but also like she's taunting me. She'll get her reward if she keeps this up.

I clear my throat. "One of you will follow us into that room." I point at the room in the back, behind the stairs. It's the room where I sat by the fire the other night, and none of the girls have seen it yet. I bet they're wondering what the hell will go down there.

Oh ... if only they knew.

Smiling, I let my eyes travel until I find the first girl.

"Britt."

"What?" she stammers.

"Come with us," I say, holding out my hand.

"Wait. Why aren't you telling us what's going to happen?" Latisha asks.

I smirk. "Are you that eager to find out?"

The moment I say this, she shuts her mouth again. Of course, she doesn't have the balls to object.

None of them know what's going to happen next, and judging from the way she's trembling, Britt's terrified of this very idea. Not knowing what comes next can sometimes be a blessing ... or a curse.

"I ... I ..." she stammers, tears welling up in her eyes as she steps toward me.

"No," Naomi suddenly interjects.

I frown as I watch her step forward and push Britt back. "I will go first."

"Hmm ... now, this is interesting," Anthony says, smiling from ear to ear.

Motherfucker.

"You want to go first? When you don't even know what will happen to you?" Anthony muses. "How brave of you."

"Or maybe she just wants to get it over with," Devon says with a laugh.

I don't tell them what I'm thinking, but it's neither of those two options. She's only doing this so she can win. So she can be the first to do whatever's necessary to get her hands on that prize ... the marriage and the money.

"Thank you," Britt mumbles to Naomi.

She only nods. Of course, she's not doing it for Britt. Naomi isn't empathic, even though I imagine her pretending to be just for the sake of staying alive and keeping the peace. After all, a vicious catfight is the last thing she wants when she knows she's the top-ranked bitch in the house ... and those girls have claws sharp as a razor.

I've experienced it firsthand with Lauren.

The stinging on my arms draws my attention. I pull up my sleeve slightly to check my skin, which has scratch marks all over it. Then I realize that I was talking and that Naomi was looking.

I quickly lower my sleeve again, but her fox eyes tell me she's seen it.

Will she realize what I've done?

A brief smile is all I get before she grabs my hand and says, "Let's go."

I smile back. "All right. You'll be our first."

I lead the way, while Devon and Anthony follow us into the room underneath the stairs.

She looks around the room as I lock the door behind her and then stand in front of the table near the fireplace.

I beckon her to come closer.

She does so with calculated steps, not taking her eyes off me for even one second.

When she reaches me, I step aside.

"On the table are three objects," I explain. "They represent my brothers and me. Choosing one means excluding the others. One of us will have you as their personal plaything for one day. Now ... choose wisely."

I wink at her, and as I pass her, I briefly caress her right shoulder.

I don't do it without rhyme or reason.

It's a clue.

And I hope she chooses right.

My brothers and I walk past her as we all stand behind the table and watch her gaze at the items in front of her. The first is a crop. The second one is a noose. The last one is a knife.

Her fingers slide along the table as she stops at each of the items, carefully examining them. She stops at the knife and gazes at it intently.

"Don't even think about it ... it's blunt. And besides ..." Anthony flashes his holstered gun, which she only briefly acknowledges, before returning to pacing around the table again.

Her steps slow down until she pauses.

Right in front of the noose.

Her fingers reach toward it. My heart momentarily stops beating.

When she touches it, Anthony calls it.

"Mine."

With parted lips, she glances at me, but before she can say a word, Anthony has her by the wrist and drags her out of the room.

I grind my teeth, grab the knife off the table, and throw it at the wall. "Fuck!"

"Jesus, she got you good, didn't she?" Devon muses.

I smack my fist on the table. "Dammit. Why the fuck did she pick the wrong one?"

"We didn't tell her which item belongs to who. Duh."

"I know!" I run my fingers through my hair. "But she should've picked mine!"

"You just don't like to share. Well, too bad, bro … this is how it goes. These are the rules." He shrugs.

I shake my head and sigh out loud, feeling the tremors in my fist. "I'm going to kill him if he hurts her."

"Who cares?" Devon throws his arm around my shoulder and pulls me along. "Let's go get the next girl."

12

Accompanying Song: "The Demon Dance" by Cliff Martinez

Naomi

Anthony holds my hand as he guides me up the stairs. The girls downstairs all watch me as he leads me away from them, some of them scrunching up their faces in fear. They don't know what comes next, but I do. One by one, they'll be pulled aside and lured into that room to pick an object that belongs to one of the men.

I wonder if one of them will get more girls than the other. If they'll become jealous of each other.

If so, then this is definitely a good game for me. I picked the right one to toy with Max.

I knew his item was the knife. It was obvious, judging from the way he was winking at me and then touching my shoulder. But today is not his day.

I also knew the whip meant pain, and since Devon liked handing it out, I already figured that one was his. The only one left was the noose ... for Anthony.

I knew exactly who I was picking ... and why.

I'm going to mess with Max's mind. Just like he did with mine.

Make him crazy jealous. Make him think I'm going to die. And then ... he'll protect me from his brothers at all cost. Hell, he might even kill them for me.

I clear my throat and smile at Anthony as he smiles at me. He's so chivalrous, the way he lets me go first and holds my hand while he leads the way. It's like he wants this to be special. Romantic. Or maybe it's all one big trap.

When we enter his room, I'm amazed at the serenity that it exudes. A white linen bed sits in the middle, which rests on a dark block of wood. On the ceiling, a fan gently blows cool air downward. White sheets cover the dark brown windowpanes that line the walls and let the light in but block the view from the outside. The walls are cream-colored and minimalist. To the right is a beige leather chair with metal chains attached to it.

I suppose this isn't just a room where he sleeps.

He pulls me into his room and sets me down on the chair, carefully arranging my hands and legs to fit neatly. Out of nowhere, he caresses my cheek and tucks a strand of my hair behind my ear.

Then he shackles my feet.

A sudden rush of fear overcomes me, but I remain quiet as he walks off to his cabinet and places the key on top. He opens a drawer and pulls out a zip-tie.

"Lock your hands together," he says.

I do what he asks, and he puts the zip-tie around my wrists, tightening it until I can't move anymore.

A voice from downstairs calls out. "Anthony! It's time." It's Max.

Anthony smiles at me and presses a soft kiss on my forehead. "I'll be right back."

He walks out and closes the door behind him, leaving me all alone in a room that feels like a soundless, timeless cage.

I listen to the rhythm of my own heartbeat and the gasps from my nose as they increase in frequency. I wonder what he will do to me. If it's going to be as bad as what Devon did to Lauren. If it's going to be worse.

It takes so long for him to come back, I don't even know how much time has passed when he opens the door again, but when I see his face, I am honest to god happy. Happy that I'm not alone anymore, even though it's sick and twisted. Because who would want to be alone with a guy like him?

Except we're not alone. Not anymore.

Britt's holding his hand now.

She looks surprised, confused even, when she sees me strapped to the chair.

But she doesn't say a word as he guides her to the bed. "Lie down on your back."

Funny how he never asked either of us to undress first.

Or maybe it's utterly terrifying.

She does what he says, and he attaches her feet to shackles that were at the edge of the bed, which I failed to notice as we came in. Then he grabs another zip-tie from his cabinet and uses it to secure her wrists, only this time they're tied to a pole at the head of the bed, so she can't move her body.

He smirks as he leans over her body and caresses her cheeks too, tucking her blond hair behind her ears. Her pearly blue eyes focus on mine for a second, and I wonder if she's scared.

He slides off her again and goes back to his cabinet ... only to fish out what looks like a ring gag.

I watch as Britt begins to struggle while he crawls on top of her again and says, "Open your mouth."

"Please—" she begs.

He interrupts her. "Do as you're told." His voice is sultry, dark ... dangerous.

Reluctantly, her lips part, and he uses the opportunity to slide the ring gag inside and attach it to the back of her head. Now, her mouth is forced to stay open, and when she tries to talk, I can only hear gurgling.

He grins. "Don't talk. It'll only make a mess." He rubs some spit off her chin and onto her cheeks. "Don't close your eyes."

He gets off her again, and his eyes hone in on me. In a few seconds, he's towering in front of me. "Unzip me."

I do what he asks, but the zip-ties make it difficult.

"Take out my cock," he commands.

As I flip down his boxer shorts and his already-hard cock flips out, a sense of power rushes through me. I could hurt him really badly right now ... but I don't because I play nice. I play by the rules. I play to win.

With his palm on the top of my head, he forces me to lean in. "Make it wet."

I spit on his cock and rub it in nicely.

"That's it … keep jerking me off," he growls.

I go back and forth across his length, keeping in mind that he's just another brother waiting to be pleased. If only Max were here to witness this. I'd die to see the look on his face, the defeat, the rage he felt over my betrayal. His prized possession jerking off another guy.

"Faster," he says.

I follow his command to the T, watching his face to see what he likes.

After a while, he closes his eyes and starts to moan.

His hand reaches for my face, and he covers my mouth and nose with just one hand, making it impossible to breathe.

"More," he growls.

With two hands, it doesn't take long for his veins to pulse and his cock to bounce.

His hand drifts down to my neck, allowing me to breathe again, but only for a few seconds … because as he wraps his fingers around my throat, he begins to suffocate me.

"Keep going," he moans as his fingers tighten.

I struggle to breathe, my hampered breath sounding like a squeak, but I keep jerking him off.

The pressure of his hand releases, and I suck in a heavy breath. One glance at Britt and I can tell she's freaking out.

Anthony turns his head, brings his finger to his lips, and shushes her without saying a single word.

Then he focuses on me again and wraps both his hands around my neck. "Don't stop what you're doing … make me come."

I do what he says, even though his hands cut off my

126

airway again.

It's not just sexual. I could handle that … but this … this is something else. I can see it in his eyes.

He gets off on seeing the lights switch off.

Near death turns him on, and it terrifies me.

The only way I can keep going is by imagining I'm jerking off Max.

My power drains the longer he squeezes, and the more he does it, the more powerless I feel. But I can't give up. Not now. Delirious and all, I continue to jerk him off, even when I'm on the brink of losing consciousness.

I part my lips in a desperate attempt to regain air.

To regain my life.

Before I pass out.

I can't breathe.

"Fuck, I'm coming," he groans.

In my head, Max says that … And Max is the one who comes all over me.

A splash of warm cum jets onto my face. It lands in my mouth and all over my chest and clothes. It just keeps coming and coming, and my hands move on their own to milk out every last drop.

In the end, when I'm almost gone, he releases me.

Air finds its way back into my lungs, and I suck it in like no tomorrow.

God, no wonder they didn't stipulate safe words in the agreement. There's no such thing as safety with these three brothers.

I take a few seconds to recover while Anthony smears the excess cum from his dick on my face. "You look stunning when you're out of breath." His finger lingers on my lip. "On the brink of destruction. So beautiful."

He smiles that wretched smile again, the one that could win hearts if I didn't know what a devil hid underneath his façade.

Then he walks off to Britt.

She squeals her lungs out as he approaches her, but it's no use. He crawls on top of her and sticks his dick into her mouth, which is held open by the bit. She twitches and struggles underneath him, trying to get him off, but to no avail.

I can only sit here and watch the whole ordeal. I'm still sucking in air like it's the final breath I'll take. I never realized just how much I'd miss breathing until he took it away from me. God, that despair I felt. Just the reminder of his hands wrapped tightly around my neck makes my throat clamp up again.

I don't ever want to feel that way again.

And if he tries … so help me god, I *will* kill him.

I don't care how, but I will make it happen.

Britt's desperate eyes catch mine in a moment of kinship, but I look away. I can't bear to witness the fear in her eyes, especially when he starts choking her too. The sounds she makes are awful. I wish I could plug my ears … that I could turn everything off and just disappear, even if only for a moment.

He plunges in and out of her mouth, and I swallow away the slickness of his cum that lingers on my tongue. He keeps going, smearing his cock all over her face and mouth until he's hard again. It makes me wonder how long this whole ordeal will last. If he'll go on all night. If he'll continue fucking me next. How many times will the cycle repeat?

One thing I know for sure … I won't take this a second time.

Picking his item was a bad idea. Maybe I shouldn't have tried to outplay Max, and then I wouldn't be in this position in the first place. It also explains why Max seemed so angry when Anthony walked off with me as his prize. Perhaps, it wasn't just jealousy. Maybe he feared what his brother would do to me like I fear for my life right now.

Anthony continues to fuck her mouth and strangle her until she fades in and out of consciousness, only to repeat it over and over again. She spits and gurgles, her eyes teary, and her face covered in saliva. It's a mess.

I don't know how long he continues like that.

Minutes. Hours.

Time has vanished for me … maybe for all of us.

This room does something to me. To him. It makes us all crazy.

After a while, I'm so thirsty my lips have started to chap. My body is trembling, but I refuse to ask for help. Doing so would mean drawing attention from *him* … And I'll do anything to prevent that from happening.

Suddenly, Anthony roars out loud like he did with me, and he thrusts into her mouth with such fervor, I can hear her choke from the size of his cock.

"Take it! Take it like a good girl," he growls.

The cum slips from her mouth, but he uses his dick to wipe it back in again.

"That's it. Now, swallow it all," he murmurs.

When he's done, he smears the excess cum and saliva all over her face and crawls off her again, leaving behind one big mess.

"Be right back." He buttons up his pants again and leaves us alone.

It takes me a second to realize this.

We're on our own.

I've been waiting for this moment for hours on end.

"Oh, god …" Britt mutters, her whole body covered in goo. She bursts into tears.

I don't have time to console her. I have more important things on my mind right now … like escaping.

Somehow, I find the energy to pull my arms up and gaze at the zip-ties. They're not too sturdy. Perfect for an escape.

I bring my arms up and whop them down hard. My wrists hit my body, and the zip-ties fail to hold. Finally released.

I quickly check my feet to see if I can get them out as well. Too bad the shackles are made of some kind of metal, which can't be easily broken. However, I do spot the key on the cabinet near the door. I guess he forgot to take it with him in his hurry. *Perfect.*

"What are you doing?" Britt mumbles as I start hopping away with the chair still attached to my body.

"Getting us out of here," I say as I use all the energy I have left to hop from one side of the room to the other.

"But … isn't that against the rules?"

I ignore her obvious fear of being caught because it's honestly the least of my problems right now. I need to get that key before Anthony comes back. Before he finds out what I'm trying to do and decides to kill me on the spot for defying him.

When I'm finally there, I snatch the key from the cabinet and ram it into the lock, finally freeing my ankles too. I jump up from the chair and catch myself on the cabinet. My balance sure took a hit after that heavy choking session.

I shake it off and rush to Britt with the same key. "Let's hope this works," I mutter as I stuff it into the locks around her ankles. It clicks. "Lucky."

Footsteps are audible from down the hallway. "He's coming back," she hisses. "Hurry!"

"I'm trying!" I retort as I struggle to free her from the zip-ties. In a last-ditch effort, I run to the cabinet and rummage through his things until I find a credit card. I use it to pry open the system that holds the zip-ties around her wrists together.

"Got it," I mumble as they release. "C'mon."

I help her off the bed, but she seems so drowsy and out of it that she can barely stand. "Hold onto me," I say, as I put my arm underneath hers to provide support so she can lean on my shoulder. I don't know why I'm doing all this. Maybe it's because I know how bad it felt to have him do that to me ... I feel sorry for her. How could I leave her here when he could come back at any moment?

I might be a cold-hearted bitch, but I'm not frozen. Yet.

We stumble to the door, and I prop Britt against the wall so I can open the door.

However, the moment I grab her again and we leave the room, we come face to face with Anthony.

He's holding a pitcher with water, and the first thought that goes through my mind is slurping up every last drop. The chance he'll give it to us now that we've escaped are very slim, though.

"God-fucking-dammit!" He smashes the pitcher against

131

the floor, splintering it into a million tiny pieces.

We squeal and run the other way, while Anthony yells, "Not so quick!"

He rushes into the bedroom and comes out with a cat o' nine tails leather crop with spiked ends; something I'd imagine you'd use to torture someone. And he's coming straight toward us.

"Run!" I push Britt forward as Anthony catches up with us.

But she's not strong enough to walk on her own because she stumbles, and I feel like she's going to fall. So I stay with her, determined to get her out safely, even if it means getting hurt.

And boy … does it fucking hurt.

One whip lash to the back and I'm squealing in pain. "You're not going anywhere!"

Gone is the romantic man who charmed every girl into saying yes.

Gone is the sexual deviant who wanted to take our breaths away.

Only the monster remains now, and he's coming for us.

"I'm not done with you yet!" he yells.

"But we're done with you," I reply, standing my ground.

"How dare you? I thought we were having fun," he growls.

"Being choked to death is not my idea of fun," I answer. I whisper at Britt, "Don't look back. Keep walking."

He hits me again, and this time it feels like a fire lights right on my skin. I hiss from the pain, but I still help Britt down the steps. I won't stop. Not now that I've finally gotten out of his grasp.

"What do you think you're doing? You can't defy me."

"Stop me," I growl back.

He hits me again, but I can handle the pain now that I know what it feels like. There's no way I'm going back to that room. He can drag my dead body back if he wants to.

"These are the rules: You stay, and I do what I want to your body."

"I'm allowed to leave and cancel the contract at any point in time," I reply, taking more steps.

He follows Britt and me. "Are you? Because then you can kiss your fifty million goodbye."

I take a few seconds to answer so I can take a few more steps with Britt too. "No."

He roars out loud. "What an insult! You dare to escape my room *and* break our rules? I'll kill you if you leave!"

The whip cracks on my back once more, but the pain doesn't even faze me anymore.

"Want to kill me? Go ahead," I say. "But nothing, and I really mean *nothing*, is going to stop me from getting away from you."

"You want to die already?" There's a smug smile on his face.

I push Britt down further and say, "Go. I'll be right there."

"Answer me! Are you that eager to die?" he yells.

"I'm not afraid of death. But you know who is? You," I sneer as I take another step. "And you wanna know why? Because if you dare to hurt me any more than you already have … your brother will kill you for it."

"What?" He makes a face.

"Max. Don't you know he wants me more than anything

in this entire world?" I narrow my eyes the moment I see the flicker of doubt in his. "I know he does. I've seen the way he looks at me. How possessive he is over me." I take another step, but he doesn't lash out. "If he finds out what you've done, he's going to be mad as hell."

I watch him swallow, and when I take another step, he doesn't follow us anymore.

I was right.

He is afraid of death … and I am all that stands between him and his brother.

And it's exactly where I'm supposed to be.

13

Accompanying Song: "Are We Having A Party" by Cliff Martinez

Naomi

That same night

After we escaped Anthony's grasp, we immediately went back to the women's bedroom to recover. I helped Britt shower and dress, after which I took a shower myself. I didn't dare shower with her, for fear she'd see my wounds and feel guilty. Or worse ... she'd see them as a weakness.

Drying off my skin hurt, as the lashes were still fresh and felt like cuts running all the way down my back. Still, I managed to put on a dark blue dress that runs all the way down to my feet. It's not something I'd wear every day, but we're in a competition, and I'm still in it to win.

Despite the fact that Anthony took a bit of my power away from me, I didn't lose myself, and I don't intend to. Not as long as I still breathe.

It amazes me that Anthony didn't come after us. I expected to have to fight him off at the door, but he never even followed us further. I wonder if he went to his brothers instead. Maybe they're talking about ways to cancel the contract ... or to kill us.

I shake my doubts off and walk the hallway to the nearest balcony I can find. I need some fresh air.

The moon and the stars in the sky are shining brightly, and they are so clear without all the city lights to block them. It's actually quite nice. I never thought I'd say this, but I don't even miss the city. The only thing I miss is my freedom ... but I'll get that back soon.

Footsteps behind me make my glance over my shoulder.

"Did I scare you?" Max asks, smiling like a real gentleman, even though he isn't.

I turn my head away again, staring at the sky. "No."

"Hmm ..." He stands beside me. "You do know I can tell when you're lying?"

"How do you know?" I ask, gazing at him from the corner of my eye.

With his elbows, he leans on the balustrade. "You always do this thing with your eye ... it twitches."

"Oh ..." I suppress a smile and look at his arms, which still show the red scratch mark. It was there since before the last game, so it must've been from Lauren. It's the only explanation.

"You saved Lauren, didn't you?" I say.

He licks his lips, but he can't suppress a quick smile.

"What gave you that idea?"

I point at the scratch marks, which he quickly hides under his sleeve. "Oh, this … I just scraped the wall. That's all."

"Right …" What a little white lie.

It's quiet for some time, and I just stare at the stars, wondering what this all means.

"You know … you have the most beautiful eyes I've ever seen," he says. "Can I ask … what's your descent?"

I smile. "I'm a quarter Japanese, a quarter Vietnamese, and half American."

Max chuckles. "Quite the mix."

I nod. "Yeah …"

"Still very beautiful if you ask me."

"Thanks." I don't want to blush from his comment, even though I do.

Suddenly, I feel his finger on my cheek, caressing me softly. It makes me want to lean in when I shouldn't. His finger travels down my neck to my shoulders, where he slides my dress down and exposes my wounds.

His eyes flicker with rage.

I hiss when he touches the lashes, and I immediately pull my dress back up again. "Please, don't," I say.

"Sorry," he says. "That must hurt a lot."

"It's fine," I lie. Of course, it's not fine, but I won't admit that to him.

"It doesn't look fine to me."

"Yeah, well, you can thank your brother for that." I clear my throat.

Max steps closer and grabs my chin, forcing me to look at him. "Hey … I *won't* let him hurt you again."

The way he says the words, with such determination, makes me suck on my bottom lip.

"How do I know you're telling the truth?"

"If it were up to me, you would've never gone to his room. But you chose his object." Max makes a fist with his hand, and for some reason, it gives me pleasure knowing my choice upset him … that he wants me so badly he'd be angry with his brother for stealing me away.

Max cocks his head and grabs my arm, pulling me toward him. "You did that on purpose, didn't you?"

I swallow but don't reply.

"Hmm …" He smirks. "Figured you wouldn't tell me the truth. You want to see how far I'm willing to go to get you?" He leans in closer, his lips almost touching mine. "You think I'm playing you to betray you, but you're wrong. I want you more than any other girl."

"Why should I believe that, when I know you've been sleeping around with the other girls? Who was it? Jordan?"

He raises his brow. "As a matter of fact, yes. And Lauren."

Just the thought makes me want to lash out.

But it also means that Asya, Latisha, and Stacey must have picked Devon's item. Oh, boy.

"Jealous?" Max sneers.

I shrug, even though I am. "I don't care."

He squints. "Of course, you do. Why else would you ask?"

"To make a point. *They* were with you. Not me. Them. So why should I believe you like me more?"

He scowls at me. "They chose my object. If you'd done the same, you'd have been one of them."

I roll my eyes. "Oh, exactly. *One of them*. Like that's some sort of privilege."

"Don't you understand that I'm the only one here who gives a shit about you?" he growls.

I try to shove him away, but he won't let me go, so I slap him instead.

He releases me from his grasp, and I step back, watching him with a hawk's eye. He touches his face with his hand, his fingers grazing his beautiful skin, and it's at this moment that I feel most vulnerable. Most afraid. Because whatever he's going to do or say next isn't good, and it's my fault.

"I ..." I stutter.

He comes toward me, and I stumble backward until the balcony is right behind me and there's no way to flee. He's got me cornered, and his eyes predict thunder, but I'm afraid I can't handle the electricity.

I close my eyes, expecting the inevitable.

Instead, he grabs my face with both hands ... and he kisses me.

He fucking kisses me.

And I don't even fucking pull back.

What the hell?

His lips smash into mine, and he ravages me without holding back. I'm helpless to stop it—not because I can't, but because my body doesn't want him to stop. His tongue dips out to lick my lips, coaxing me to open my mouth and let him in. I do, without hesitation, and he claims my mouth and tongue like it's always belonged to him.

I'm completely stunned. I can only stand here and allow him to conquer my mouth, even though it makes no sense. I should hate him for putting me through all this. I should push him away and fight back. But I don't ... and I hate that more than I hate anything.

In a moment of clarity, my lips unlock from his, and I lean away, staring at him because I can't believe that just happened.

I'm not exactly the kissing type ... but that was amazing. And wrong. So fucking wrong, I might've even liked it.

"I told you I only want you. It's the truth," he whispers, his voice heady and sultry. My lips still tingle from his kiss, and I can feel the excitement surging through my body. Goddammit.

"I don't give a damn if you slap me. I probably deserved it."

I grind my teeth but don't respond. I wouldn't know what to say anyway. Apology or no apology, he is right ... He deserved it.

He grabs my hand and brings it to his lips, kissing the top of my hand. "I can't undo your choice, but I can give you what you need now that you're back."

"Back ... from his room you mean," I say with bitterness in my voice.

"Yes," he says, narrowing his eyes. "I must say I'm impressed you managed to escape. May I ask how you did it?"

"Like I'll tell you all my secrets," I retort.

He gives me a lopsided smile. "I suppose you're right. Still, I find it intriguing."

"So you're not mad I defied your rules?"

He shrugs. "If my brother loses, he loses."

I frown. "Aren't you all about punishing the girls who don't listen?"

"Yes, but your punishment was to deal with my brother when you didn't pick my item." There's a smug smile on his face. "It was the knife, by the way. Good guess."

I fold my arms. Clearly, he's letting me off the hook when he wouldn't give the same privilege to the other girls. I don't know whether to be upset or proud. He really has a thing for me.

"This is just how the game goes," Max explains. "Although I have to admit that seeing you here on the balcony with your dignity intact makes me happy."

"My dignity, yes ... my body, not so much," I say with a sigh. "I hope for your sake these don't turn into permanent scars. Otherwise, you know what's going to happen."

His lips quirk up momentarily. "The added clause to the contract." He smiles. "Clever. Did you incite my brother?" He inches closer again. "To *make* him hurt you? Is that your plan? Because if it is, I can tell you it's a bad plan."

"No, of course not." I lift up my head and gaze at him from under my lashes. "But I told him he couldn't stop me from leaving. And when he threatened ... well ... let's just say the moment I mentioned your name, he stopped chasing us."

His eyes narrow, and a hint of possessiveness sparkles in his eyes. "You mentioned my name and told him I'd kill him."

So he knows...

His brother must have told him that I ran, but I guess Anthony didn't tell him how he whipped me.

"You think you can use me against my brothers?" Max asks; although it sounds more like a statement.

It's wisest not to respond to that, so I don't. I just look

away at the horizon again.

It's quiet for some time before he interrupts the silence again. "You're a smart woman, Naomi."

"Thank you."

"But you should know not to mess with me or my brothers." He looks me dead in the eye. "People could get killed."

I wonder who he means.

"Is that what happened to Camilla and Hyun?" I ask.

He makes a face and laughs. "No, of course not. Why would we? They may come back and rejoin our game."

"Right." I sigh. "More girls."

"Tell me the truth …" He leans against the balustrade like me. "You don't like to see me with the other girls, do you?" Before I can reply, he already has that wicked smile on his face again. "That means you want me for yourself too."

I close my eyes and sigh out loud. "Max …"

He slides my hair aside and whispers in my ear, "I love it when you say my name. I want you to say it the first time I fuck your brains out."

My pussy clenches with need.

Fuck.

"Is that what you told them before you fucked them?" I mumble.

He muffles a laugh. "I never even touched them." He sighs. "I only talked with the girls and gave them something to drink."

"Really?" I scoff.

"Yes," he reiterates. "Like I would be interested in fucking them after seeing you run off with my brother." He

142

shakes his head. "Why do you always have to question everything? Can't you just accept that I want you?"

I close my mouth and wait a couple of seconds before I come up with a reply. "When you stop asking questions ... that's when you're no longer alive."

He chuckles and blinks a few times. "I wonder then ... now that I've told you what I did with the girls, what did you do with Anthony?"

I frown and look away. "He shackled us to chairs and zip-tied our wrists."

"Who's we?"

"Britt," I say. "And then he proceeded to face-fuck us while suffocating us. One by one."

Max's face tightens, and the look in his eyes reminds me of lightning striking down on earth. His hands turn into fists, and he smashes them onto the balustrade. "Fuck!"

"Jesus, you'll hurt yourself." I quickly grab his arm and pull it away.

"Now you suddenly care?" he barks, jerking his arm away.

I'm baffled. I don't know how to respond. Part of me wants to say of course, but that would break the illusion of my aloofness. It would make me vulnerable, and I hate having any weakness, let alone showing it to him.

"I'm sorry; that was rude," he says after a few seconds, and he caresses my back with his hand. Too bad it only makes me hiss from the pain. "I'm going to have to take a look at your wounds."

"No. I said it's fine. I showered. The blood's gone."

He pulls down the back of my gown with ease. "You don't want to get an infection. Oh god ..." He pauses and gazes at the marks on my back. "You're right. I am going to kill him."

He briefly glances at me before rushing off.

I follow him to his brother's room, where he screams, "Anthony. Open the door!"

A few seconds later, Anthony casually opens the door, only for Max to punch him in the face.

I hold my breath as I watch Max jump on his brother and stomp him to the ground. He smacks him repeatedly, screaming at his face.

"You fucking hit her with a whip!"

"She ran away! It's against the fucking rules!" Anthony yells.

He punches him in the stomach, and they roll around on the floor. Anthony's a lot bigger than Max is and quickly overpowers him, rolling on top.

"Stop fucking hitting me!" Anthony almost chokes Max as he tries to hold him down.

"I'll kill you!" Max kicks him in the balls so hard his brother falls to the ground, and he proceeds to hit him again. I never realized how intensely satisfying it is to watch two men fight over you ... and see them bleed, of course.

I just watch them tumble around, fighting like two grown-up kids. I don't feel the need to interfere. They both had it coming, and I must say ... it does feel nice to see Anthony with the bruises he so deserves.

Suddenly, a scream is audible from the floor below.

The guys stop fighting and look up.

Another scream. "Help!"

I run to the balustrade and gaze across. Stacey comes out of a hallway to the right, looking for us, so I yell, "We're here!"

She turns her attention to me, the shocked look on her face making me clutch the balustrade. "What's wrong?" I ask.

"S-something's wrong with Asya. Please, s-someone, help," she cries, tears streaming down her face.

I nod and turn around, whistling at the guys who stop fighting each other. "Asya's in trouble."

The guys get up immediately, their faces red from exertion, but neither of them cares. As we rush through the hallway, following the screams to the women's bedroom, they don't even look at each other, and not a single word is spoken between the two of them. They're completely focused on getting to the girls as quickly as possible, just like I am.

Stacey trails behind us, sniffling. When I open the door, I find Lauren on the couch, clutching herself, while Jordan, Britt, and Latisha all huddle near the window, all extending a hand.

To Asya.

Who's standing in the windowsill, staring down at the earth below.

My eyes widen as we all come to a screeching halt in the middle of the room.

For a brief second, Asya turns her face to us and stares blankly. Her face is white and partially covered in blood. Her lips parted, streams of blood pouring out. The look in her eyes reminds me of death.

"Please, come down," Latisha begs.

Jordan tries to grab her hand, but Asya pulls away, inching closer to the edge.

"Stop," Max growls.

Asya doesn't even blink as she opens her arms and lets her body fall back.

The sound of screams as her body tumbles to the ground shocks me to my core.

Thud.

14

Naomi

Three girls down, six left.

The girls huddle together for support, their sniffling and whining driving me crazy mad.

I can already barely deal with my own mind spinning stories, never mind the whimpers audible in the back.

"She said she was done with it all," Stacey mumbles, clutching her blanket. "I can't believe she's gone."

"Me neither, but I do understand," Britt says. "I mean she said she'd been thinking about it for some time. She told us."

"Yeah, from what I heard, her parents told her to basically get married or die trying," Stacey adds.

"Whoa," Jordan mumbles, sipping her tea.

"Yeah; no wonder she was so on edge."

"Not just that, but then she chose Devon's item ... and she lost it the moment she found out. She grabbed the knife and tried to throw it at him, which failed to hit its target. He didn't take it too well. At least, that's what she told us," Latisha says. "She was the first to be tied up and lashed. I could hear her screams all the way from down the hall, and that was before I knew I had picked his item too."

"Yeah ... gosh ... there was so much blood when he was done with her. He barely even looked at us," Stacey says.

Latisha nods, staring into blank space. "I would've liked to know what else he could do. I mean we're here to marry one of them, so we might as well try them all out and see which one fits us the best. Even though I like Anthony the best," she says with a giggle. "But it's too soon to choose."

She talks about the men like they're shoes you try on at the store.

Pathetic.

The other girls stare at Latisha, who quickly adds to her story. "What? I mean there are three of them, and I think we should keep our options open. Besides, we all have our favorites." She raises her brows. "Devon only tied us up and used some toys on us, like vibrators and crops." She shrugs. "And he likes to fuck asses a lot." She ends it with a small giggle that's barely noticeable.

"When you're not prepared, yeah," Stacey says.

Lauren shivers, probably remembering how he tied her up and used her.

"He went easy on us because he'd already wasted his energy on her," Stacey says, grabbing a pillow to hug. "I'm happy I survived. One of us wasn't so lucky …"

The girls nod and stare off at the window and then down at the floor. Talks like these are never easy. What do you even say to each other after you've just watched someone kill herself? Nothing adequately describes what we all witnessed. Nothing.

I'm sitting in bed, trying to think, but all I hear are their voices as they shout about how unfair it is. Why she suddenly decided to jump. How she died for nothing. That it's cruel. Who they can blame for it all.

While all I can think about is how many more of us will perish before they have their way.

Is this why they offered us the fifty million dollars?

Not just to be their concubines, but because there was a possibility we could die?

Goose bumps travel up and down my body, and I shake them off. It's quiet in the room, too quiet, and when I turn my head, I can hear the sound of a bag zipping up.

The baggers … people Max called to clean up the mess and make it like it never happened.

He explained that they'd tell her parents she died in a freak accident during her vacation and just wipe away her very existence in this place. And when they're done, it'll be like she never even existed.

I shake my head. What money can buy you still scares me sometimes. Not that I should be surprised; they managed to get to all of us so easily. It's a wonder they even care about the contract. They could've just kidnapped us instead. But I bet that's all part of the game they play. After all, where's the fun in taking what you can already have freely? It's much more fun if it comes to you instead.

The talking dies out slowly. As nighttime approaches, the girls push their beds toward each other and come together for support. I'm the only one who doesn't need to be cuddled as I fall asleep.

However, in the middle of the night, whispers in my ear wake me.

"Naomi …"

I turn around and see Max holding his finger over my mouth. "Don't say a word. Just come with me."

I take his hand and let him take me from my bed and out of the room. When he shuts the door, the girls are still fast asleep. Max holds my hand firmly as he pulls me downstairs and into the room with the red bed sheets again, where he opens another door into a private bathroom.

He turns on the bright lights and beckons me. "C'mon. I won't bite."

I step inside the bathroom and look at my own reflection in the mirror. Max stands behind and places his hand on my shoulder, sliding aside my hair. At first, I think he's going to kiss me, but he carefully slides his fingers into my nightgown and the thin bands around my shoulder, pulling them down one by one until the nightgown drops to the floor.

I'm naked in a room alone with him, and I wonder if this is the moment he'll take me for himself. He's been craving it all this time; I know it, and I can see it in his eyes. The hunger when he sees my naked body. I can feel it from his fingers, softly trailing down my back. It's electrifying. Dangerous.

"Are you going to take what's yours now?" I ask.

He gazes back at me through the mirror. "Is that what

you want?"

I swallow away the lump in my throat, not knowing how to choose between two possible responses. One is a lie ... the other is the truth.

He smirks. "It's okay; you don't have to answer. I won't make you do anything you don't want to. Yet."

That last word spreads goose bumps all over my body.

He pulls open a cabinet to the left and grabs some sort of lotion, which he pours into his hands. Then he starts to massage it onto my back slowly, carefully crossing over the wounds on my back. I hiss from the pain, which makes him go even slower and softer. Not a word is spoken between us as he rubs it into my skin. The look in our eyes speaks volumes. He knows what I think of him ... but he doesn't care, and I know he doesn't.

He's here with a purpose—a goal in mind—and that's to take care of the wounds his brother inflicted. Even though bruises and cuts cover his own face, he's solely focused on me now. As if he's trying to repair what's broken ... trying to keep together the tainted picture of perfection.

Despite the fact that a girl just died.

***

Accompanying Song: "Eyes On Fire" by Blue Foundation

MAX

"How can you live with yourself?" she suddenly asks.

I cock my head but continue to scrub her, this time a bit harder. "Easy. Just shut everything and everyone out."

"That's avoiding the truth," she says.

"The truth is someone died. It happens."

"It happens ... so it's normal to you?"

I stop with the lotion and put it away. Questions like these are hard, and I don't always have an answer to them. "It's never normal to watch a girl die."

"Then why didn't you do anything about it?" When I turn around, she's facing me, still naked, her nipples peaking like she's cold. She's beautiful, perfection itself, and I can't help but wonder how they would feel in my hand while I kissed her until morning.

Not now, Max.

"I couldn't," I say, letting out a sigh. "She'd already made up her mind."

"You knew?" Her eyes widen.

I close my eyes. "We talked about her parents and how they wouldn't accept her back. She wanted to leave but couldn't. I told her there's a place here for her. She said she didn't want any of this, and that she was going to leave. That's all I knew."

I go to my knees and lift up her gown, pulling the straps back on her again. That way she's much less of a distraction to my eyes. Still, they can't help but wander off from time to time, trying to get another peek at her body that's so ready to be mine.

"Why did you let her leave your room then?"

"Because my brother came to me," I explain. "And he told me about you, so I came looking for you after telling the girls they were free to go."

"And then we went to Anthony," she says, frowning.

"Yes."

She closes her eyes and sighs. "Someone just jumped out of a window, and you're massaging my back with lotion."

"It's not just lotion; this helps to prevent it from getting infected."

"Someone *died*," she reiterates, clearly angry.

"Yes, indeed, and no matter what I do, I can't change that fact. I can only clean up the mess that's left and give her a proper grave." I clear my throat. "However, what I can do is help those who are still alive. Like you." I place a hand on her arm. "I know it's tough to accept, but I do care about you, despite what it may look like."

"You care about me because I'm to become your wife."

I smile. "Yes, indeed. Make no mistake, you *will* become mine, and when you are, I will take proper care of you. You won't have to wish for anything because you'll have it all. Life can be good with me by your side. All you have to do is accept it."

She jerks away. "I can't believe we're talking about this now."

I grab her wrist as she tries to walk away and pull her back to me. "Stop fighting. Stop resisting me. I know you feel what I feel."

"Money isn't worth dying over ..." she spits.

"No, but marriage is. Especially when it comes to marrying the most beautiful, smartest woman I've ever met." My index finger brushes her cheek, and I lean into her ear. "I need you by my side, Naomi."

"To be your wife ... but you do realize marriage is also

about love?" she murmurs.

My thumb lingers on her lips as I'm reminded of the last time I kissed her. I can still remember the way she tasted … like heaven.

"I already love every little bit about you."

She laughs and shakes her head. "Oh, my god …"

"I'm serious. I love your scheming. Your devious little ways. You're just like me—cunning, not afraid to stand your ground—and I adore that."

I wonder if I should kiss her.

If my brother did when he had her.

If he touched her in places I have yet to discover. Doubt eats away at me as I think of how he's tainted her. I want to erase him from her mind. Replace his mark with mine. And I *will* make it happen … no matter the cost … no matter how long it takes me to get to that point.

"Why don't you go for the easy girls? The ones who really want this?" she asks.

"You're lying to yourself now," I muse. As I lean in, she steps back against the sink, and I cage her with my arms. "You have no idea how valuable you really are. How long I've waited for a woman like you. Someone who I can not only marry but who will also be my equal and give me something no other woman can." I smile when I see her blatant death-stare.

"If only you knew," I mutter.

"Knew what?" she asks.

I bite my lip. Should I even tell her?

If I do, she'll scheme more and maybe try to overthrow me in my own plan. Then again, if I want her by my side, maybe I should let her in on the details.

However, if my brothers find out ...

"I won't tell a soul," she adds.

Narrowing my eyes, I wonder if that's a lie or the truth. This time it's hard to tell, but I suppose telling her might make her trust me more. Maybe then, she'll finally see things from my view. I need her by my side, and she needs me. End of story. It's time she knew just how important she was.

"We didn't just bring the girls in to fuck them ... to find out if one of them is the one we want as a partner ... a bride," I say, my lips so close to hers I can feel her breath on my skin. I look her deep in the eye and swear to myself that I will kiss her right there and then. Because when she finds out ... it may be our last time.

"It's to find out who we could see ourselves with forever ... and to make an heir." Her pupils dilate, and her breathing stops. "A baby, Naomi. And I *will* be the one to impregnate you."

15

Accompanying Song: "Sweet Dreams" by Emily Browning

Naomi

"Wait, what?" I stammer in complete and utter shock.

Babies.

This is all to make babies? Heirs?

Suddenly, he presses his lips to mine, taking me by surprise. I'm overtaken by the sudden kiss, which feels too good, too surreal. I can't let him get to me. Not now. But he won't stop, so I bite his lip.

He draws back and touches his bloody lip with his fingers. "Ouch. Is that what I deserve?"

"Kissing me after telling me *that*? Really?"

He seems unapologetic. "Yes, really. Especially after that. For all I know, you could be gone in the morning now that you know. I just had to kiss you one last time … if it is."

I lick my lips to try to get rid of his taste, but it only makes me remember how good of a kisser he is. Goddammit.

"Why tell me? Why now? And why not the other girls?"

"Because I want you as my mate," he says, stepping closer again.

"Whoa, whoa ... hold your horses ... mate?"

"Yes, to make a baby. That's why we need to marry."

"Jesus." This explains everything. The need to test us. All of the games that involve fucking. It's not just to find out who the best sexual match is ... it's to get us pregnant.

"Heirs to what?" I ask after a few seconds.

"Our company. Our father wants us to marry and have a kid. It's tradition. This is how it went for him, and now, it's how we do it."

"Your father ... You do this all because he wants you to?"

His nostrils flare. "We have no choice in the matter."

I blink a few times and take in that information, forcing myself to remember that for later. It's important because it could mean that his father is his enemy too ... and I can use that to my advantage.

"So that's why we're here ..."

"This was all planned a long time ago, Naomi. You and I were meant for each other." He grabs my face just below my chin and pushes me against the wall. "I want your pretty lips ... your pink, flushed cheeks ... those beautiful dark eyes that haunt me ... that body I'd die for... that mind I'd kill for. I want it all, Naomi. And I want to see it in my child. All of it."

He inches closer and smells my skin like some kind of animal. "I've never craved a woman as much as I crave you. What is it about you that makes me so desperate? So needy?" he growls, and he stomps the wall beside me, making me jolt up and down briefly. "So fucking violent ..."

I know what it is. It's infatuation but telling him is no use. He already knows the answer to his own question. Just like I do.

"What are you going to do now?" he murmurs.

"I don't know yet."

"Are you going to leave?" He licks his lips and stares at mine like he wants to ravage them again.

God, if I let him, I know I'll be hooked for good.

"Thanks for the lotion," I say, and I push past him and walk out.

"Naomi," Max calls out, but I don't turn around. "Don't go."

It doesn't sound like a question.

It sounds like a command.

One I might listen to ... but I'll sleep on it before I make my decision.

I make my way back to the women's bedroom and sneak across the floor as quietly as I possibly can. Latisha snores as she rolls over, probably disturbed by my entry. However, she doesn't look up or even speak, so I guess she's still asleep.

I quickly go to my bed and crawl under the blanket, where I can safely think about what I just learned.

Babies.

We're here to marry and make babies. Like real fucking concubines.

Wow.

I can't believe this is real. I wonder if the guys do it because they want to … or because their father forced them. Maybe the company is due to be taken over by one of the guys, and he's trying to decide which one to pick. If it's the latter, I can definitely see the real enemy here. It would explain why the guys are in such a hurry to get married and fuck all the girls on the premise. Three weeks to make sure you win.

If I'm right, this is one monster of a bomb.

One I'm not sure I'm willing to share with the girls.

Max would probably allow me to tell them, but do I really want to, when there's so much at stake? If I win—if I marry Max and get pregnant—I will get half his share of the company. It's quite a lot.

Still, it doesn't explain the rivalry between the brothers. It's like they fear they'll get kicked out if they don't win this game quick enough. Like their father will do something crazy if they don't marry and make an heir.

It's a possibility.

I should ask next time I talk to Max. If I ever do.

Because let's face it—I'm very tempted to go home after all that's gone down lately. I'm just not sure if the money is still worth it. Doubts are chipping away at my otherwise absolute resolve, and I don't like it one bit.

The girls will probably find out later on anyway … it's only a matter of time. I'd just rather have it later instead of sooner. They are my competition, after all.

Guess I've decided then. No sharing from my side.

Accompanying Song: "I Am A God" by Kanye West

MAX

Day 12, evening

Anthony sits across the room, as far away from me as he possibly can. We haven't made up after our fistfight, and I don't intend for that to happen either. He crossed a line when he put his hands on her and hurt her. I won't forgive him.

Still, we can't keep our eyes off each other. Probably because we're both thinking of ways to kill each other. I can tell from the way he flips the pages of his book and sips from his wine that his eyes are boring a hole in my head.

Devon leans back in his chair and burps after taking a long sip of his beer. He laughs a little when he looks at me and then at Anthony. He picks up the cue and walks to the pool table, playing the balls by himself.

Then he grabs a cigarette and lights it, blowing smoke in my direction.

"You two look horrible. Got into a fight?" he muses.

"Shut up," Anthony mutters.

I don't respond.

Devon grins. "Suits you well."

"I said shut it," Anthony barks.

"What? It's not my problem you two can't keep your

damn heads straight."

"What are you talking about?" I mumble.

"That girl's playing you both, man," he says. "Naomi. She's trying to get between us. Can't you see?"

"No," I say. "Anthony tried to fucking kill her."

"No fucking way I did," Anthony growls. "I was teaching her a lesson. The rules are there for a reason. She defied me, so she got punished."

"You didn't have the right to touch her!" I yell. "She's *mine*!"

"Did you forget this is a three-way deal? We're all in it together," Anthony muses.

"Not when she has a special contract that allows her to take over my fucking shares of the company if she gets any permanent scars."

"That's on you for including that, not me. Not my circus, not my monkeys." Anthony takes another large sip from his wine glass.

"Fuck you," I mutter.

Devon laughs again. "You're hilarious, guys." He takes a second drag from his cig. "I'm so fucking glad I found some girls who have exactly what I need and aren't already claimed by you whiners."

I roll my eyes. "Yeah, right ... like any of the girls would want you after realizing what you love."

"What? One of them actually likes the fucking pain." He shrugs. "Not my problem you don't believe me."

I narrow my eyes. "Who?"

"Latisha."

"Really?" I frown. "Hmm ..."

"Yup, she's a kinky motherfucker."

"You think she's got a thing for you, but she's got a thing for all of us. She just loves sex. That's all," Anthony retorts, looking away.

"Right. Whatever. Doesn't matter. I like Lauren too." Devon smirks and takes another drag. "Anyway, the point is … just get a fucking grip. Get a girl. Get married. Get it over with."

"You forgot the last step …"

"Oh, right." Devon points at me. "The fucking baby!"

"It's not as easy as you think."

"Like I care," Devon sneers. "I'm only in it to get Dad on my side."

"As if he'd ever choose you," Anthony sneers.

"Fuck off," Devon retorts.

"You know he meant what he said," I say. "About the whole heir to the throne thing …"

Both of them look at me now, like it's so fucking unbelievable that Father would be speaking the truth.

Anthony mulls it over a few seconds before he opens his mouth. "You think Dad would go to that extreme to get the best one of us?"

"Yes," I answer. "Without a doubt."

They both know what I mean.

I get up and go to the kitchen, grabbing three glasses from the cabinet. I pour some whiskey in them and then grab a small tube from my pocket. I take out two pills and drop them into two of the glasses, letting them dissolve. With this dosage, it's sure to mess with their swimmers. Especially if I continue with this dose every day. And they won't even notice something's wrong until it's too late. How convenient.

162

With a smirk on my face, I walk back to my brothers and set the glasses down on the pool table.

"What we all need right now is a drink."

They glare at me suspiciously.

"Like you said … we're brothers," I say, looking at Devon. "We shouldn't fight each other. Although, you can be sure that I will defend my right to Naomi," I say while looking at Anthony. "C'mon."

The guys approach me, and I pick up my drink and hold it up. "To the Wicked Bride Games."

They both toast with me, and then we all drink up.

It's hard, so hard, not to smile this wicked smile.

Like I said … I'll do anything to win.

***

Accompanying Song: "Sweet Dreams" by Emily Browning

Middle of the night

I wake up in the middle of the night to sounds coming from the hallway. With a drowsy head, I get up and open my door. Devon's footsteps are what I heard as he walks up the stairs, holding a bottle of whiskey in his hand. He drinks from it as he stumbles up, barely managing to stay upright.

Slipping out, I follow him as silently as I possibly can, making sure to hide behind a potted plant when he gazes around. He seems to be intoxicated, and I wonder if it's because of all the drinking or a side effect of the drug I gave him.

Still, he goes upstairs to the women's bedroom. I stalk behind him and watch him sneak inside.

I wait … and it feels endlessly long, making me feel like I should go in there and see what he's doing; maybe stop him while he's at it.

But then he comes out again… with a girl in his arms.

Lauren.

Her body is completely limp, her arms and legs hanging to the side as he drags her out.

"What the fuck did you do?" I whisper-yell at him.

He doesn't even look fazed that I caught him. "Taking what's mine."

I frown as I see him tuck away a wet cloth into his pocket. "Right …" He must've used some kind of sedative on her … chloroform from the looks of that cloth.

"And what are you going to do with her?" I ask as he drags her body through the hall.

"Bringing her to my dungeon."

I swallow at the thought of that basement and what he's done to it. "But you're wasted," I say.

"So? I wanna have some fun," Devon says as he grabs her waist and throws her over his shoulder like it's no big deal. Then he hauls her down the stairs.

"Can't it wait until tomorrow?" I plead, hoping he will listen, but I already know he won't. He has our father's genes, after all—just like I do.

"Fuck no; I want her now."

I follow him as he brings her to his lair. I call it a lair because it's where he hides half the day. He brings all his girls down there so he can use all kinds of toys and tools on them without anyone hearing their screams.

He pulls her to some chair and sets her down on it, propping her up like some doll he wants to prepare. He even tucks a few strands of her hair behind her ears and buttons up her nightgown.

"You like her, don't you?" I ask.

He turns his head to me. "Yeah ... I like her the most."

"So she's the one, huh?"

"Maybe ..." He narrows his eyes. "What's it to you?"

"Oh, nothing." I shrug, realizing this is exactly what I wanted ... For my brothers to find some other girl to latch onto. However, I don't want to leave her to her fate. "But maybe you should wait until the next game. You know ... to keep it official."

Devon just stares at me with this nasty look on his face like he knows I'm not supposed to be here.

"Father would appreciate it," I add.

"I don't give a damn about Father. I'm taking her," he slurs, and he pushes me away. "Now, get out and leave me alone!"

Before I can do anything to get her out of his grasp, he's already locked the door, and only he has the key.

Fuck.

I hope she doesn't wake up soon.

16

Accompanying Song: "The Demon Dance" by Cliff Martinez

Day 14

In the morning, we wake up to the sound of someone entering our room.

"I'm back, bitches!"

Her voice makes all heads in the room turn around.

"Oh, my god!" Stacey squeals. "Camilla!"

As the other girls jump out of bed to hug and greet her, I stay put and watch the spectacle from afar.

"You're really back?" Stacey asks.

"Yes!" They high-five each other.

"But why?" Jordan asks, frowning. "I mean … why would you *want* to return to this?"

Camilla pouts her lips. "Well, I need money; that's basically it." I can tell from the way she answers that it isn't the complete truth. Maybe she was threatened. It isn't farfetched, considering we've already lost a few potential brides. Maybe the brothers finally realized that they'll need all of the girls who are left, including the ones who don't want to be here.

"Couldn't find a job?" Latisha asks, raising her brows.

"As a matter of fact ... no," Camilla says, sighing. "I just couldn't get out of debt. After spending so much on my education, I couldn't even afford my own damn home. I needed a loan, a job, anything, but I can't get work anywhere because of this damn bad credit following me every step of the way."

"I hear you," Stacey says, nodding. "My hair salon costs thousands, and I'm still not out of debt."

I'm noticing something strange here. Are all the girls in debt?

"So you came here hoping to get back into the game." Jordan folds her arms.

"Yes. I mean ... I do fucking hate the idea, but I gotta do something. Money isn't gonna come rolling anytime soon, and this is basically the only opportunity I have. I'm screwed. But I need this as much as you do. So just so you know ... I'm ready to kick butt." She laughs and winks playfully, but I know she means it.

She's as serious as I am at winning this game. That's why I never figured she'd be the first to leave. Then again, she's stubborn as can be. Figured she would take the marriage plans hard.

I wonder what she'll do when she finds out this game's

not just about being someone's wife… It's about becoming a permanent asset to one of these men's lives.

And now that she's back, that means more competition for Max.

No fucking way I'm going to be all happy and jolly about the fact that she's returned.

However, this also means that it *is* a possibility to return. As in … the contract can be reinstated. So if I wanted to leave, I could safely do so without having to worry about losing my place here.

And I know there will always be a place here for me as long as these games are still going.

Max wants me too much. He'd never refuse.

I look around the room and gather my clothes off the floor when I notice one girl hasn't gotten up from her bed.

I drop my stuff, get up, and walk to her bed, but when I get there and pull off the blankets, there's no one.

Lauren's gone.

"Guys …" I mutter.

They're still talking with Camilla about how she spent her time away from the girls, and everything that happened so far while she was gone. They don't even hear me, so I scream.

"Guys!"

Now, they turn their heads; most in annoyance, though, but I don't care. They should know this.

"Lauren's missing," I say, and I show them the empty bed.

Their eyes widen one by one. "Oh, shit …" Latisha says. "Do you think she left?"

Biting my lip, I look around her bed, but her belongings

are still here. Who would drop everything they had and just leave? No one. It's like she never left.

And then it hits. She never did.

My jaw drops as I rush toward the girls.

"What's wrong?" Britt asks me, but I ignore her as I open the door and march down the hallway on a mission.

Down the stairs is the dungeon, but when I get there, Max appears from a door to the side and blocks my way. "You don't want to do that, Naomi."

"Get out of my way," I hiss, getting up in his face.

"Calm. Down."

"I will not calm down. I know you've got her in there."

"I don't have anyone in there," he says.

"Semantics. You. Your brothers. I don't care. Now, let me through."

"Why do you care so much? I thought we'd been through this already," he says.

"Because I have to know ... I have to know what you're capable of."

"My brother," he whispers, pointing at himself. "Not me."

My nostrils flare. "Your brother ... Devon, right? He's the one who's got her."

Max takes a deep breath. "Trust me, Naomi, you do *not* want to go in there. Take it from me."

"Wrong." I try to shove him away, but he keeps pushing back. "I want to see her. *Now.*"

"You don't care about her. You don't care about any of the girls here," he says.

Right at that moment, the others follow behind me. The distrustful looks on their faces as he says out loud what I've been thinking all this time cuts into me like a knife.

"Out of my way!" I yell and ram my elbow into his side so hard, he bucks and heaves.

I grab the chance to rush past him and ram the door open, but it's locked from the inside.

"I told you that you didn't want to go in there!" Max says as he approaches me from behind.

"Watch out!" Britt calls out in support.

But she's too late … Max has his arms around me, forcing me to stop jerking on the door handle.

"Let me go. Let me see her."

"Please … Naomi, I'm begging you, stop fighting me."

He never begs.

"Why? I want to know what he did to her. I want to know—"

His lips touch my ear as he whispers, "It'll scar you forever."

My lip trembles. "I don't care." Maybe I do. Maybe I shouldn't want to know. After all, I'm not after Devon. However, he is Max's brother, and they have a bond that goes deeper than blood. Who's to say Devon's desires won't be Max's at some point? I *have* to know what happened to her, so I know what might happen to me if I stay.

"Are you sure about that?"

After a few seconds, I slowly nod.

He leans into the door and pulls a lever on the right side, which opens a small peephole. "Go ahead … look."

I turn my head and watch the girls cower in fear, clutching each other's hands as they fear the worst. Someone has to discover what Devon did to Lauren. If it has to be one of us … it'll be me.

So I press my face against the door and look through the hole.

What I see makes my breath hitch and my heart stop.

Lauren's naked body tied to an iron bed. Blood-soaked sheets beneath her. Eyes wide open, soulless. Her breasts ... cut with careful strokes of a knife, a delicate pattern drawn on her skin in the shape of a heart. And Devon, lurching over her like a zombie, holding her hand as he weeps.

"Oh, god ..." I slap a hand in front of my mouth.

I can't believe what I'm seeing, even though I know it's true.

I should've seen it coming.

"Do you understand now?" Max whispers in my ear, pulling me back to reality again.

I shake my head. "We can't leave her there."

"It's already too late for her now. She's gone."

I turn around in his arms and punch his chest. "You could've done something!"

Max grabs my wrists and pins them against the door. "I couldn't do anything. Even though I wanted to, I couldn't do anything to stop him from being a fucking savage," he growls. "I don't have a key. He's locked the door from the inside. Why do you think I was here in the first place?"

To make him stop.

To make him change his mind about taking her for himself.

To make him keep her alive.

"I stayed all fucking night to watch over her, to call out to him, but he wouldn't stop. He wouldn't fucking stop." Max slams his fist against the door. "I told you not to look."

"I don't regret it," I say. "I know the horrors that I face

171

now."

Suddenly, I hear a loud roar from behind us, and I turn around and gaze through the peephole again ... only to be confronted with a raging mad Devon looking straight back at me.

"You ... I see you looking at me. What do you want?" he growls. "Can't you see I'm mourning?"

"Mourning?" I mutter. "You killed her!"

"I did *not* kill her!" he screams at me, his teeth stained with blood. I shiver at the thought of what he did to make them bloody in the first place. "I *loved* her."

"Love? You don't even know what that is. You're a monster," I hiss.

He smacks the door so hard I can feel it move.

"I drew my fucking love into her body; that's how much I loved her. But she had to go and leave me."

"What did you do, Devon?" Max intervenes.

"I didn't do shit!" Devon screams. "She just suddenly stopped breathing, and her body was moving up and down, her eyes rolling back. Next thing I know, she's gone. *Gone!*" He wails again like some kind of animal.

Max looks at me and mumbles, "Heart attack, maybe."

I look away and swallow the lump in my throat.

I wonder if she screamed so hard, she faded.

If he scared her so much that she stopped breathing.

If the pain became too much to handle and her heart just ... gave up.

Maybe it's better that she's gone. At least she won't have to feel any of it anymore.

With my hand on the wall, I walk back and past the girls, all of them still in shock over what they just heard.

"What now?" Britt asks.

"What do we do?" Stacey says.

"I don't understand. Devon killed Lauren?" Latisha sneers as if she doesn't believe it happened.

I reply to none of them. I don't have the strength nor the will.

This has gone too far.

"Naomi. Don't leave," Max says as he stands next to door to Devon's basement dungeon.

"Don't stop me," I yell as I walk off to get my stuff.

"You sure about that? If you leave, you might never be the same again." It sounds like a warning … or a threat. A part of me wants to know what it means, but the rest just wants this all to disappear.

"Where will you go?" His voice is bitter.

I can only give him one answer that's not a lie. "Home."

Part III
The Revelation

17

Accompanying Song: *"Are We Having A Party" by Cliff Martinez*

Naomi

Day 15

After I got all my stuff and left, I took a cab straight home. Along the way, I kept staring at the people walking around outside, thinking … if they only knew what kinds of things happen all around them.

Sitting in that cab felt like the first time I could breathe again.

Like I'd been freed of a burden I didn't know I was carrying.

And still, as I sit here at my table drinking a cup of tea, I wonder … what if I'd stayed?

Would I have won the games?

Would I have become Mrs. Marino and remained gorgeous while pregnant?

Would I have all the money and wealth I could dream of and save my father from an ill fate?

Would I be happy?

I have so many questions that doubt still lingers in my mind. Instead of answering them for myself, I just shut off my brain and proceed to read the newspaper, trying to find something to keep my mind busy.

Tick. Tock ... Tick ... ... Tock.

The ticking stops, and I look up at my clock hanging from the wall. The hands have stopped moving.

I get up from my chair and pull it from the wall, taking out the batteries. Guess they're dead. Placing the clock on the couch, I let the batteries tumble onto the table to confirm. Too many bounces. Yup. I hate it when things stop working like they always do in my home.

Time to go to the store.

I quickly put on my coat and go out, locking the door behind me as I make my way down the hallway of my apartment building. The stench that meets me from a few rooms ahead makes the bile rise in my throat, and I stop breathing for a second as I rush down the stairs to get away from it all.

This life ... the stench ... the filth ... the broken things.

It just gets on my nerves and makes me want to scream.

Out on the street, I walk down the pavement with my head down, trying to be invisible. Normally, I get catcalled all over the place, but now, I just want to be left alone. Besides, it's raining heavily, and I don't want my hair to get wet. So I pull up my hoodie and pretend I don't exist.

Except, when I turn my head, I can clearly see a black Chevrolet Equinox riding so slow it feels like it's following me.

Chills run up and down my spine as I keep moving through the crowd, trying to ignore this feeling of someone chasing me. I shouldn't even be thinking about this. I chose to leave, and it was my right to do so. Max explained it thoroughly; we could leave at any time with no obligation.

But then why is my stomach twisting in knots?

I quickly enter the nearest grocery store I can find and shake off the rain as well as my jitters.

The cashier eyes me like a fox as I search the racks until I find what I'm looking for. Batteries.

I place them on the counter and fish out my wallet. "I'll take these, please." The cashier furrows his brows at me like it's odd I just came to buy batteries. "And a pack of cigarettes, please," I add, to make it more plausible.

"Fifteen dollars, please." His voice is toneless, just like his face, as he grabs the cigarettes and takes my five and ten dollar bill.

Right then, the little bell above the door goes off, almost making me jolt. My heart beats in my throat as a random guy starts sifting through the magazine rack.

Shaking my head, I close my eyes for a brief second and tell myself to calm down.

It's all in your head.

Stop being a crazy bitch.

I shove the two items in my purse and say, "Thanks," then I rush out the store again.

On the first street to my right, I find a black Chevrolet

Equinox parked.

I stop in my tracks and gawk, but no one is in the vehicle. Strange.

Continuing my way back to my apartment, I clutch my purse even tighter and ignore anyone who crosses my path. I try to stay invisible, moving like a snake through the crowd of people walking along the same sidewalk, but when I hear the sound of tires in the distance, I can't stop myself from glancing over my shoulder ... and watch as the black Chevrolet Equinox drives in my direction once again.

I start to run, as fast as I can, with only one end in sight—my apartment. It's so close; I can almost feel it, and when my hand reaches the door handle, I don't stop even for a moment to look around. I just rush inside and slam the door shut behind me.

Out of air, I hurry up the stairs, not giving a shit that my legs are hurting and that I can barely breathe. I have to get back home. Home ... where it's safe.

When I get to my door, my hands tremble as I fish my keys from my purse and unlock the door, slamming it shut after I get inside.

Bent over, I take a moment to suck the oxygen back into my lungs. Sweat drips down my forehead, a drop falling to the floor. And at this moment, I wonder what kind of person have I become?

Paranoid? Schizophrenic? Delusional?

I don't know anymore, but I do know that I am losing my mind.

Someone is stalking my every move. I just know it. That car wasn't just there by accident. It's always there when I go out onto the street. It's not a coincidence. Who are they, and what do they want from me? Maybe they're connected to Max. Or maybe the government was onto the brothers and is now onto me since I'm now affiliated with them. Because let's face it … those contracts and what they're doing inside that house is *not* legal.

Regardless, those men outside can't follow me in here. I'm safe.

I take a deep breath and straighten my back.

Fetching the batteries from my purse, I take them out of the packaging. I flip over the clock and stuff two batteries in the container, turning the hands until the clock is reporting the right time again.

But as I lean in to hang the clock back on the wall, I notice a peculiar little thing. A small, round cap tucked away under the bottom corner of the clock. I carefully peel away the piece of tape that holds it there and then it pops right into my hand.

When I look at it closely, it's not just a random cap, though.

It has a small antenna … and a lens.

Jesus fucking Christ.

Motherfucker.

***

MAX

I sit behind my laptop with my hand on my crotch, casually sipping my whiskey on the rocks with the other. I care not about the other girls in the house. I never have. I only wanted to show them a lesson ... and give my brothers something to play with while I focused on the important task.

Seducing and making Naomi mine.

But now that she's no longer here, I've lost interest in even entertaining our guests.

During dinner, all I do is eat my food and leave the table. I don't talk, I don't visit them, and I don't go out at night. I only eat with them because I must keep up appearances.

But I'd rather stay in bed all day and night to watch my laptop while I masturbate. Without knowing I'm watching her every move, I can get off on just the image of her strutting around in her apartment.

For days, I watched her cook, clean, dress, eat, and sleep. Anywhere and everywhere she went, I was there. Not physically. Not mentally. But I was there.

Like a god ... influencing her every move.

Even now, when my people have followed her outside in the Chevrolet Equinox, they did so under my explicit instructions. It was all part of the plan.

She needed to find out.

She needs to know the truth.

And now, she has.

I've waited so long for this moment. This particular look on her face. The surprise. The realization and how I can literally see it take form. And then the betrayal.

It's magnificent. Pure magic.

Just the gaze in her eyes as she stares back at the lens makes my cock hard.

I sit back and watch her scream at the camera with a grin on my face. I squeeze my crotch with one hand while shifting through each of the cameras, making sure they all record her image and voice.

"Max ... I know you're watching," she growls at the camera.

I lick my lips as I watch her anger burst.

I love it. It's exactly how I imagined it; rage bubbling to the surface and culminating in an explosion so magnificent, it could even beat an orgasm.

"I know this is a camera. Come out and face me instead of sitting behind your screen like a coward," she yells.

My nose twitches, and I'm so goddamn inclined to take her up on that offer.

Maybe I will.

***

Accompanying Song: "Scream" by Grimes ft. Aristophanes

Thirty minutes later

181

I knock on her door three times. She doesn't respond.

"It's me," I say with a low voice.

I know she can hear me. I can tell because I don't hear her walk. She's focused on the sound of my voice and trying not to make any move herself. She has some nerves, calling me out to come to her and then pretending she's not even there.

"Open the door, Naomi," I say.

When she still doesn't reply, I shake the doorknob.

I can hear something screech. Probably a chair.

A faint smile appears on my lips. "I know you're in there."

"Why did you install those cameras?" she suddenly asks.

"Open the door, and I can tell you."

"No. I'm not crazy."

"Then why did you tell me to come here?" I ask.

"Because now, I can hear you too."

I smile to myself. "Smart."

"Tell me why." She's much closer to the door now.

"I will if you let me in." I place my hand on the door, wondering if she's doing the same.

"I can't," she says. "This is the only protection I have against you."

"You don't need protection against me," I muse.

"When the only man I thought I could trust turns out to have planted cameras in my home? Yes, I do."

I sigh. "Believe it or not, I'm still the only man who wants you safe."

"Prove it."

I frown and pull back. "Are you sure?"

She doesn't answer, which can mean only one thing. She

doesn't know what she wants. Well… I can make it much easier.

"Suit yourself," I mumble.

Then I tuck my hand into my pocket, take out a key, and push it into the lock of her door, twisting it so it opens.

18

Accompanying Song: "Scream" by Grimes ft. Aristophanes

MAX

"What the—"

Her jaw's practically on the floor.

"You wouldn't choose, so I chose for you," I say with a shrug, and I tuck the key back into my pocket.

"How did you? When?" She stumbles backward, clearly confused. So out of her element.

I've never seen her act like this. It's like she saw a ghost.

"Don't be scared," I say, approaching her. "Wait, never mind." I grin.

She almost knocks over a table but keeps it upright by grabbing it. "You have a key to my apartment. Why? Explain yourself," she growls.

"I will, if you would only calm down," I say, holding up my hands. "Stop moving so erratically. You're going to tear up your apartment."

"*My* apartment? Oh, right … this condo that you so *conveniently* just broke into."

I shake my finger at her. "Correction. Walked. I didn't break in. I have a key."

"I never gave you permission to enter."

"But you do want me to explain myself, so I kindly let myself in after pleading with you multiple times. Fair, no?" I nod at one of the chairs at the table. "Sit."

"Like I'm that stupid." She keeps circling her couch, avoiding me at all cost.

"We both know you're not. I'm not your enemy."

"Cameras everywhere and you're telling me you're not my enemy? Laughable," she scoffs.

From a small cabinet to her left, she manages to grab a pair of scissors and holds it out like a sword. "Don't come anywhere near me."

I hold up my hands. "I'm not going to harm you."

"You already have," she says.

"Where?" My nose twitches again from that claim. "Because if my mind serves me well, my brother was the one who hurt you, not me. And I am *not* my brother. How many times do you want me to tell you before you'll accept this fact?"

"You toy with my mind …" She taps her head.

Oh … that kind of hurt.

I can't help that it makes me smirk when she says that.

"That's because I like you," I reply.

"Funny way to show someone you like them," she sneers.

I make a face. "Naomi, please. Let's not resort to

fighting."

"You give me no choice. When you wiretapped my apartment, you crossed a line," she growls.

I try to step forward, but she keeps that pointy thing in my direction like it's a weapon.

"I said back off."

"I get it. You're confused."

"Why are there cameras?" she interrupts.

I slowly pull off my coat and let it drop to the floor. "So I can watch your every move and make sure you don't do anything stupid … like call the police or hurt yourself."

Her eyes narrow. "How long?"

"Long. Very … very long." A wicked smile forms on my face at the sight of hers turning white.

"And the other girls? Are there cameras in their homes too?"

I nod.

"Been watching us like a perv?" she sneers, licking her lips. "Pathetic."

My lips twitch, and I can barely contain myself as I march toward her. "Enough." I grasp her wrists and push her against the wall, making her drop the scissors. "Yes, I've been watching you, Naomi." I lean in and smell the fear on her skin. "I've watched you eat, sleep, dress. Shower." I smile and gaze at her from underneath my lashes. "I've seen you with your hand in your panties as you masturbated on the couch."

"Is this supposed to impress me?" she quips, and she tries to push back, but I shove her right back where she was against the wall.

"You told me to come; well, here I am, right where you

want me. Just like I have you right where I want you."

"Giving us a choice on whether or not to sign the contract was all a farce, wasn't it?"

I nod as she slowly takes it all in.

"You had us all along."

"I had *you*," I murmur. "I still don't care about the others."

"Why make me sign it then?"

"To give you the illusion of control …" My pants tent against her hot body. "To give you the idea that you could escape, even when there's no such thing as your life separate from mine."

"So this has been going on since …"

"Since you were only a girl," I say with a low voice.

Goose bumps scatter on my skin just from telling her that.

"What about the other girls? Did they know all this?"

"No," I reply.

"But you still made them sign the contract."

"Because we wanted them to give in to us willingly. It's more fun that way." I smirk.

She sucks in a breath. "We were groomed … to be your wives. Why even go through the trouble of pretending that we had a choice?"

"Choice, Naomi. I want you to choose me because *you* want me. I want you to beg." With my feet, I spread her legs and step between them, making her feel my hard-on. "I want you to ache for my cock." I rub myself against her, making myself even harder. "I could take it all from you whenever I want. Make you submit to me. But there's no fun in that." I lean back again and look into her eyes.

She visibly relaxes, and I release her wrists. "You wanted the chase," she says.

"Exactly." I lick my lips at the sight of her furious eyes.

"Why tell me all this? Why now?"

I raise my shoulders and lower them. "Because it was time. Simple as that."

She squints. "Because I caught you."

"Perhaps." The left side of my lips quirk up into a smile.

"Those men outside … were they yours?"

"Yes. I'm surprised you noticed them earlier too," I say.

"They didn't hide it very well," she quips.

"I didn't want them to," I whisper. "I like to see you all riled up."

"You made me lose my job, didn't you?" she hisses.

I close my eyes and nod. "I gave you that job … and then I took it away."

She balls her fists. "And the rent? All those bills that stacked up and just kept increasing?"

I nod again.

"Even the refusal of the banks to loan me any money?"

With an unmoving face, I say, "All of it."

Out of nowhere, she lifts her hand and smacks me across the face. Again.

My skin glows like hers, and I can still feel her handprint on my cheek when she's lowered her hand again. I contemplate strangling her right there and then. But that would be such a fucking waste of a smart, beautiful girl who I want to fuck so badly.

I just go for it.

I smash my lips against hers, kissing her with no regret. I do it because I must. Because some part of me can't hold back and needs to fix what was broken. Then again, I also do it because I'm a sadist fucker who just gets turned on by her rage.

A hot flash and a bloody lip follow. I touch my mouth again as she shows me her teeth, her lip pulled up, so sexy it hurts.

"That won't stop me, Naomi," I say. "Nothing will."

I grasp her wrists, pin her to the wall, and kiss her again, pushing my body against hers to make her feel how much I want her. I won't let her run away. I won't let her escape. Not after I just told her the information she so desperately sought.

I'm not one for sharing, but if that's what it takes to make her trust me, then so be it.

From the way she kisses me back, I can tell it's hard for her to resist too. Our mouths lock in a battle of lust and wits, neither of us able to quit the other.

Her lips are so tantalizing; I could lose myself in them. And as my tongue dips out to lick her lip, she pulls back and says, "I'm gonna smack your head against that wall so hard …"

I grin against her lips and reply, "I'd love to see you try."

She growls, but I silence her with another kiss.

"You fucking watched me like a stalker …" she hisses between kisses, but she doesn't fight back.

"I watched you because I'm obsessed with you. From the very beginning, I've wanted you. You're the one."

I grab her face and kiss her harder, but she responds by grabbing my nuts and twisting them. I groan. "I left your fucking home for a reason."

"You left because you couldn't handle the truth.

Because you think I'm like my brothers. I'm not fucking asking you to marry them," I growl, shoving her back to the wall while blocking her arms. "You're gonna be *my* wife, and I don't fucking share."

"Your brother already touched me," she hisses, trying to bite my arm.

Even if her teeth sink in, it won't faze me. The pain only turns me on.

"Trust me when I say I'd like to rip his head off for that. Unfortunately, that's the game we play. But as soon as you get pregnant, it'll all be over, and you'll ... be ... *mine*." I flip her around and plant her face against the wall. Grabbing a fistful of her hair, I pull her head back and kiss her neck fervently.

Her fingernails scratch the wall, and she shudders as my lips roam her skin.

"I can't even leave this game if I tried ... can I?" she growls.

"Not a chance." I grin and press my mouth against her shoulder, leaving my mark. "I'm not letting you out of my sight."

"So I'm a prisoner in my own home ..." she murmurs as my hand slips between her thighs and under her skirt.

"Is that such a bad thing when you're with me?" I say.

She doesn't reply; all she does is huff as my fingers pull aside her panties and grab her pussy. "This pussy is mine," I growl. "Not my brothers', not yours ... *mine*."

I flick her clit as I press myself against her body, making her feel my cock tenting through my pants. The more I touch her, the less she's struggling, and her body grows weak in my grasp. I use the opportunity to yank off my tie and throw it away, along with a few buttons, which spring loose from my reckless behavior.

I've got her pinned against the wall, her pussy getting all wet as she moans.

I know she wants this. She doesn't have to say it. I can feel it from her trembling body.

"You leave the mansion, this is what you get," I growl. "Me telling you everything just to make you stay."

"You wanted me to discover those cameras?" she retorts.

"I don't fucking care. All I want is for you to fucking finally submit," I say. "And I'm not fucking waiting anymore until you beg."

I grab her and pull her to the table beside us. In one fell swoop, I've managed to throw off a vase and a few magazines, and they scatter on the ground. But I don't give two shits. I'm only interested in one thing.

Fucking. Her.

She scratches the table in an effort to pull herself up, but I hold down her back with the palm of my hand.

"Don't fucking move, Naomi. You know you want this," I growl as I rip down my zipper and unbutton my pants.

First, I shove two fingers up her pussy and make her gasp. That'll teach her to fight me. She's nice and wet, just the way I like it.

I circle around inside, which makes her knees weak as she starts to quake against the table.

"See? There's no use in resisting. Sexual urges are natural. It's time we gave in to them."

"What about the game? Your brothers?" she mutters.

"Screw the fucking game." I smack her ass, which makes her jolt up and down. "And don't you mention my fucking brothers while we're here. Got it?"

When she doesn't respond, I grasp her hair and pull her head back, making her hiss as I slap her ass again.

"I fucking hate you so much."

I smirk. "Likewise."

Then I ram my cock into her tight pussy.

She moans out loud, the sound making my cock pulse with excitement.

God, I should've done this a long time ago.

"Fuck, you're so fucking wet," I groan, slamming her body against the table as I fuck her.

"Fuck you," she hisses.

"Focus, Naomi. You know what I want."

"As long as you get what you want, right? What about me?"

I muffle a laugh and ram into her again. "You'll get your fair share. Don't worry." I cup her pussy with my hand and start flicking her clit again.

"I meant the contract," she says, leaning up. "If I can't escape it anyway, then I want my fucking money."

"You'll get your fucking money," I growl, "but first, you'll get my fucking cock. Now, bend over." I push her down again and thrust into her violently. It's like I'm fucking every inch of rage out of me.

"Fuck," she moans as I circle her clit with my fingers.

I lean over her. "You like it when I fuck you, don't you? Admit it. Tell me you've been yearning for this," I whisper in her ear.

"Admitting is like defeat, and I don't lose," she

murmurs.

I smirk and lick her cheek as I fuck her raw. "I get your pussy, you get my cock. As far as I see it, we're both winners here."

"Fuck me," she moans.

"Harder?" I ask.

"Fuck, yes." Her voice sounds like she's nearly there, so I bury myself deep inside her and make her feel my cock pulse.

"Say my name, Naomi. Say it."

"Fuck me, Max," she mewls.

With my hand, I spread her cheeks and stick my index finger up her ass. She squeals with excitement.

"Fuck! What the f—"

"Don't pretend you don't like it," I say with a grin as I swivel around in her ass. "This is just the start."

"Holy shit …" she murmurs as I pound into her pussy and do the same to her ass with my finger. After a while, I add another one, which only makes her moan louder.

"You're a filthy whore, aren't you? The neighbors can hear you."

"Asshole."

"Keep calling me names." I smack her ass. "But you know you're only my sweet whore and no one else's."

I fuck both her holes until I find her open enough. Then I spit on her, take out my cock, and shove it up her ass.

She screams from both pain and pleasure, and I use the opportunity to grasp her mouth and stick my fingers into her. "Can't handle my cock?" I growl.

"Fuck you!" she groans as I thrust into her ass, applying more spit as I go.

"Make no mistake, Naomi … *all* your holes are mine … including your ass." I smack her again, and another moaning squeal escapes her mouth. Exactly what I like when I'm pounding into her. She's so damn tight, and when I stick my fingers into her pussy, I can feel her body contract. I know she likes it.

"Fuck, c'mere," I growl, yanking her off the table by her hair. I push her down and force her head over my cock. "Open your mouth."

When she does, I immediately shove my dick inside, fucking her mouth with ferocity. I can't control myself any longer. Her slick tongue feels so nice as it swivels around my cock, and I can feel my balls tighten.

"Suck it hard," I groan, still holding her hair.

She does it so well that I almost come, but that's not the plan. I take my cock out and pull her back up, pushing her over the table again. There, I fondle her pussy, stroking her clit until she moans out loud.

"I'm not gonna stop fucking you until you scream for me to make you come," I say, as my fingers play with her clit.

"Jesus …" she moans. "Just do it."

I smack her ass, which makes her bob up and down.

"Beg!"

"Please … fucking make me come."

Her pleading voice pushes me over the edge, so I pull my dick out and shove it into her pussy again. "Yes, fucking come, now!"

Her body convulses, her muscles contracting around my dick. I can feel every inch of her orgasm, and the sheer pleasure of it makes my cock explode.

194

A loud howl escapes my lips as I spurt my cum inside her, one thrust after the other. The jets of cum just keep coming; it doesn't seem to end. Only after four times of ramming my cock back into her do I feel fully sated, fully liberated of my own needs.

Bringing my fingers up, I smile a wickedly delicious smile as I taste her on my lips.

Such sweetness from such a passionately wild act should be a sin.

19

MAX

I help Naomi off the table and ask, "How's your back?"

"Awesome. Especially after this kind of wild sex," she retorts. "Why do you ask?"

"I just want to make sure your back is healed before I take you back."

I bring her a wet towel from the bathroom. "Clean yourself up."

"Thanks," she says, snatching it from my hand.

"And gather your things."

She sighs. "I suppose I have no say in the matter."

I look around her room, wondering how on earth she would choose this home over mine. "No."

"So the contract was false?" she says. "You know that's illegal, right?"

"It's not false, and the clause you added still stands," I say, looking at her as she puts on high heels. "As I said, the contract is there to make you feel safe. To make you *want* to be in our home and be ours. But ... even if you did want to fight the contract out in court, you'd never win. Our lawyers are the best of the best. They'll play you off as a lunatic."

"Your company is huge, right? Because I know you and your whole family are bankers," she says.

My brows furrow. I don't even know why she brings this up in the first place. "How do you know?"

"You never denied it, so I just assumed. Guess I'm right," she says with a smug look on her face.

My nostrils flare. "Yes. We own an empire," I reply.

"That means that if your little game gets out, it'll be the end of the entire business. Doesn't matter if you go to court or not. The media will have your head."

"It *won't* get out," I say with a threatening voice, so she won't get the wrong ideas in her head. "Like I said, we'll make sure of that. If any of you spills ... you'd be written off as insane. Delusional. Do you think we're stupid? We have connections everywhere, and we practically own the media," I scoff. "Besides, you'd probably be dead before you could even try. We're watching you on camera, remember? We know everything you do." I swallow. "And to answer your question ... The contract is still very much in place."

She swallows, mulling it over. "This game ... it's never been a choice to begin with. You set all of this up from the beginning."

"Me personally?" I say. "No."

"Then who?" She cocks her head.

197

I narrow my eyes, and then I grab her bag and start collecting her clothes myself. "We'll talk about that some other time."

She grabs a few shoes and clothes, but I can see from the way she's stealing glances at me that she can't stop thinking about it. "It's your father, isn't it? He decides everything."

Her comment, which sounds more like a statement than a question, makes me stop in my tracks. I wish she couldn't see right through me. To this day, I wonder how she does that. It's amazing.

"You should be thankful I'm allowing you to bring your belongings. Normally, we wouldn't. You already have everything you need at the mansion."

"Normally ... there's a *normal*?" she scoffs. "So this *has* been done before. Interesting. I thought you were joking when you said 'ages,' but now, I'm starting to believe this whole insane plot."

"No ..." I sigh. "I never said—"

"You did, technically," she says with a smug smile.

My nose twitches again. She always knows more than I expect. "You want me to tell you the truth? Because last time I did, you tried to run away from me."

"A girl died. It's not like it can get any worse, right?" she asks.

I ignore that blatant stab. "My father had the same marriage game."

She stops packing. "With his brothers?"

"Yes."

"Hmm ..." She doesn't say anything else. Just a hum. *Dammit.*

I want to know what she's thinking.

Not that I think it's good to tell her everything. She's too smart. Too savvy. She'll start playing games with me instead.

"Time's up," I say, and I grab her bag, which is still partially open, and pull it away. "Let's go."

I grab her by the arm and take her with me out of the apartment. Downstairs, the limo is already waiting for us, so I throw the bag in the trunk and open the door for her to step inside.

"How chivalrous," she jests.

I bend over and grab her chin, forcing her to look at me. "I may have fucked you like an animal, but that doesn't mean I'm not still a gentleman when it comes to you." I press a kiss on her lips, and she doesn't fight me back. I'm the first to pull away. "And you're still the only girl I want."

She raises a brow. "You sure you haven't fucked any other girls while I was away? You know ... because it's so boring without me."

I smile wickedly and whisper in her ear. "I jerked myself off to the camera in front of you... and you didn't even know it."

Then I shut the door and walk to the other side.

As I slide in, I tell the driver to go and settle beside her. She turns her head away and stares outside, not moving an inch as I scoot closer. She seems cut off from the world, lost in her own thoughts.

Even a slight brush across her arms doesn't get her to look at me.

"Are you mad at me?" I ask.

"Yes," she says.

"Why?"

"Because I hate not having a choice. You took my independence away from me."

I frown. "Interesting ..."

"What?"

"That you didn't mention me fucking you." I shrug when she looks my way. "I thought, if anything, that would make you angry."

"Not at all." She looks at her nails and bites off a piece. "Sex is just business as usual."

A smug smile spreads on my lips. "I'm glad you see it that way." My hand finds its way to hers, and I entangle my fingers through hers. "But I will keep kissing and fucking you until you see it as more than just a business deal."

"How could I possibly when there are other girls who could still win this game?"

"They stand no chance against you." I kiss the top of her hand.

"They do if your brothers pick me first," she says.

"Over my dead body."

"Really? You would die before they got their hands on me?"

"That's the game, honey, and I play to win."

"What if the girls decide that, in order to get to you, they have to eliminate me?"

I make a face. "That won't happen."

"How do you know?"

"Because none of them know what I told you."

She narrows her eyes. "So none of them know they could die and lose their money?"

"No, and none of them were smart enough to make the

same deal you did."

"Hmm ..." She mulls it over a bit and then looks away again.

"If you want to know, they haven't even thought of the possibility," I add. "The girls. They don't discuss elimination. Only leaving. They barely even mentioned you."

Now, she's the one to make a face. "What do you mean?"

"Well, I suppose they didn't really care whether you were there or not. They only seemed bothered by their own inability to come to terms with our game and their role in it. You know... whether they should stay or leave."

"Right." She bites her lip. "So they don't care."

"I do." I squeeze her hand.

"I know; you've told me many times," she replies. "But the fact that they don't care about me at all makes this so much easier."

"Makes what easier?"

She stares at the palm of her hand and slowly makes a fist as she speaks. "Not thinking of the consequences of my actions as I win this game."

I smirk at her comment and gloat to myself about her being back where she belongs. With. Me.

"You haven't won me over yet, though ..." she suddenly muses.

I suck on my bottom lip and fumble around in my pocket, wondering if now's finally the right time to show it to her. Maybe I should. Since we're being honest and all.

So I take out the necklace with the locket and hold it up for her to see.

"What's that?" she mutters. "Wait." Her fingers slip

through the necklace, and she touches the locket. "I recognize this."

"Go on," I murmur.

"This used to be mine. How did you get this?" Her eyes are wild, on fire.

She tries to snatch it away from me, but I pull back just in time. "I got it from your *real* parents."

"Real ... parents?" she repeats. "Excuse me?"

"Don't play me like a fool. I've kept an eye on you since we were kids. I know you're adopted, and you know it too."

"They are *still* my parents," she hisses. "Just because they're not my blood doesn't mean I don't love them to death."

"And I'm sure that love is mutual," I say.

She grasps the locket from my hand and looks at it intently. "This used to be mine. I remember wearing it. Why do you have this?"

"I've always had it. My father gave it to me. Said it was trash, but I decided to keep it."

"How did your father get *my* locket?"

I lick my lips and sigh out loud. "Because he killed your real parents in order to obtain you."

She leans back as far away from me as she can, staring at me like she's seen a ghost.

"Killed ... my birthparents."

"Yes," I say. "My father chose specific targets. The smartest, brightest married couples he could find and waited until they had kids. My father believes we should get the best of the best. No other women would be good enough for us ... so he opted to steal away the babies of these couples who were perfect in his eyes and put them in new

202

homes." I gaze at her. "Your adoptive parents."

Her jaw drops slowly. "My parents are part of the game?"

"Yes," I say, but then I hold up my finger before she flips out. "But not in the way you think. You know your parents weren't able to conceive. My father did too. He found them in the medical registry of the hospitals. They keep a record of couples who are unable to conceive for research purposes. Anyway, my father gave you to them in exchange for a deal."

Her eyes lower as the information sinks in. "You made them promise they'd give me to you without complaints." Her eyes widen, and she focuses on me. "They know I was sold, that I'm now in this contract with you? And they knew about the cameras, and that you and your family were keeping an eye on me this whole time?"

"Yes." I smash my lips together.

"Well, shit." She stares off into the distance. "Are mine the only ones he killed? Or were the other girls' parents killed too?"

"No ... just yours," I say. "The others all agreed to give up their child. Some of them didn't even ask for compensation. Only yours were ... difficult. They didn't accept money, not a single dime. I suppose that's where you get your stubbornness from." I swallow. "When my father realized your real parents would never give you up, he killed them instead." I point at her hand. "That locket you're holding is the only thing left of them."

She looks down at it and then clutches it harder.

It's silent for a few seconds, and I find it hard to deal with.

"Say something," I say.

"What am I supposed to say? Honestly, for the first time in forever, I feel like I could cry."

"Then cry," I respond.

"No." Her nostrils flare. "You did this. All of this."

"My father did. And his father when he started this all."

"But you continued it. You knew, and you never once thought of coming to tell me?"

"I couldn't. It's forbidden."

"Fuck forbidden." She throws the locket at me and looks away, but not before I can clearly see the tears being pushed away.

I pick it up from the seat and hold it close, wondering if it means so little to her that she could just chuck it away. Or maybe it means so much to her that she couldn't bear to look at it one second longer.

"Don't be upset," I say. "I'm only telling you the truth. That's what you wanted, right?"

"My parents are liars," she whispers. "They lied to my face ... my entire life."

"They didn't do it because they wanted to." I grab her hand. "You should know that. My father gave them a small percentage of shares in our company to keep their mouths shut, and if they did talk ... they wouldn't be alive today."

"I don't understand. I thought they were poor," she says. "*We* were poor."

"They are because they can't touch the money until you're married to one of us," I say. "My father added that as a clause."

Her hand slips from mine as she covers her mouth. "Why are you telling me this? What's in it for you?"

"You. You're in it." I smile.

"No." Her brows furrow. "There's more to this. Your father. You've mentioned him so many times." Her eyes flicker with something ... hopeful. Mischievous. "You need a girl to have a baby ... because your father wants to have an heir. But it's not just the baby. It's one of you," she murmurs.

My heart beats in my throat.

"It's not just us. You ... your brothers ... only one of you can win the ultimate prize." Her lips quirk into a devious smile. "The company."

Narrowing my eyes, I push the locket into her hand, close it, and look away.

"You not answering means I'm right," she says.

"And here I thought you were on the verge of crying," I muse. "Guess the conniving girl is back."

"She never left," she retorts. "You know, I'm starting to think all of this that you and your brothers and your father are doing is illegal. Maybe I should call the cops?"

I laugh. "Good luck ... they're all in our pocket. We contribute a lot of our earnings to the police departments. It keeps us off their radar."

The limo stops, luckily, and I take a quick breather as I step out.

Jesus fucking Christ.

From emotional to cold-hearted bitch, she can switch with the snap of a finger and not give a damn about anything in the world as long as she's the one winning.

This woman is insane.

I smile as I walk to her side of the limo to help her out.

Like I said ... a perfect fit.

20

Naomi

Later that day

"I'm back," I say, as I walk into the women's bedroom.

They're all sitting on the couch and look up at me, but after a quick hi, they continue chatting away. Their lack of surprise at my entry doesn't faze me.

I throw my bag on my bed and sit down, staring at the locket that's still in my hand.

I can't believe Max had this. All this time, he had it, and he never told me.

Maybe he was afraid of how I'd react.

I admit I almost fractured, for a moment … I almost punched him in the gut and jumped from the vehicle.

Almost.

However, when I thought about everything that he'd told me, something clicked. When I realized he was a pawn in this game just as much as I was, I knew that I still had a chance to get out on top. To get everything I want and punish those who've done me wrong. It seemed like a futile dream before, but now, it could be a reality.

All I need to do is beat these women.

And that's easy ... now that I know how to play this game.

I look around and notice that one of the girls is missing. Latisha.

"Where's Latisha?" I ask.

"With Anthony. Why?"

Interesting. "Oh, no reason," I reply. "Just wondering why we're not complete."

"She's been hanging around him a lot lately," Britt muses. "I think she's got a thing for him."

"Yeah, but I'm not so sure it's mutual," Stacey says.

"Stop gossiping," Jordan says, sighing. "It's giving me a headache."

I shrug and sit down on my bed to tuck some of my stuff back into my nightstand. I'm not just sitting here instead of on the couch because I enjoy the silence ... it also gives me the time to think about the fact that Latisha is the only one missing from the group, and that she's probably all over Anthony as we speak. I wonder if they're just talking or actually fucking. If he's already chosen her or just likes to fool around.

Regardless, it means there's little chance for the other girls to get a hold of him ... unless they get pregnant.

Someone knocks on the door and opens it right away. "Get ready, girls. Fifteen minutes." It's Devon.

I guess the next game is about to start.

I get up and walk to the bathroom to refresh myself.

Stacey's putting red lipstick on Britt's lips with utter precision. "Stay still." She grabs Britt's arm and holds her as she meticulously works the lipstick like she's painting on a canvas. Britt smiles, and they gaze at each other awkwardly as I walk behind them and open the faucet to splash some water on my face.

"All done." Stacey smiles as she tucks the lipstick back into her pocket. Then she grabs a few strands of Britt's hair and clips them behind her ear, taking great care to make her as perfect as she can be. And the way Britt looks at Stacey makes me feel like she's admiring her.

"You look beautiful," Stacey says, as her fingers linger near Britt's face.

I grab my mascara and start applying it, at which point Britt glances quickly at me and then clears her throat. "Thanks." She blushes and turns, and they both walk off like they're in a hurry.

I shrug and casually apply my makeup, knowing full well that at the end of the day, it'll all probably run down my face.

I look at the woman in the mirror and wonder what I'm becoming. If I'm ready to face these three men again. If I could let all of them fuck me again and again until I'm wasted from cum. If I could kill.

Because I have thought about killing them …

And the girls.

But what kind of person does that make me?

A monster. Precisely what I judged Devon for.

Maybe that's why Max likes me ... because I'm just as cunning and just as devilish as he and his brothers are.

No wonder they were fighting over me.

I shut the powder box and gaze at myself once more before I turn around to put on a new dress and finish up.

I've already made my decision. I'm staying, and I'm playing to win.

All the women are sitting on the couch or on the chairs facing each other. Blatantly staring. None of them speaks a word.

But I know what they're thinking.

They all know why they're here.

What's at stake. Money. Power. A company so huge it could destroy entire economies with one command.

Now that they've seen the possibilities and the consequences of marrying one of these men, they've made their choice.

None of us will give up the fight.

And none of them is willing to let the other win.

All five women go outside, and Latisha joins us as we line up in the hall again.

This time, Max is the only one who comes up to greet us. "Welcome, ladies. And welcome back to some who renewed their contract." He nods at me and Camilla, who then throws a glare at me, which I ignore.

"It's time for another test. This one is more about endurance. How long will you last?" A sly smile forms on his face. "Come join us in our game of wheel of fortune." He points at the doors at the beginning of the hall behind us that lead to the dining room, and we all turn around to see

Devon and Anthony opening them.

"Follow me," Max says as he leads the way.

The women tread behind him obediently. I'm the only one who walks beside him, not caring whether this is the way it's supposed to go or not. I know what I can expect, but I also know my place ... and it's *not* behind him, of that I'm sure.

When we enter the dining room, I hear the girls behind me gasp.

I'm not surprised.

The large twelve-person table has made a place for a bench that could fit one person ... and there are hooks and straps on the side and front.

I swallow at the sight of the bench, but also at the fact that behind it is a wooden wheel with pictures of our faces on it.

"Oh, my god ..." Stacey mumbles.

I gaze over my shoulder to see her grasp Britt's hand in fear.

"Don't be frightened," Anthony says as he pats the bench. "This here is where all the fun begins." I want to rip the smile off his face. "Let me explain what's going to happen. One of us will turn this wheel. When it lands on the picture of your face, you'll be the one to lie on this bench. But don't think you can avoid having to lie here because all of you will get a turn. We'll continue this game until *all* of you have had your fill."

He licks his lips before he proceeds. "When you are chosen, you will strip down naked, and we will strap you to the bench. Then Devon, Max and I ... will fuck your orifices."

More gasps are audible from behind me.

"The goal is to please us until we come. However, after three minutes have passed, a clock will go off, which means we will switch positions." The smirk on his face makes me want to hurl. "It also means that you will have one cock in your pussy, one cock in your mouth, and one cock in your hand. Now … the fun part is knowing that one of us will come in your pussy and one of us in your mouth."

"Without protection?" Jordan asks.

Devon laughs at her. "Don't worry, love, we're all clean here, and we know all of you are too."

I don't think she wants to know how they know, so she shuts up immediately.

"But can't we get pregnant then?" Stacey asks.

"Yes." Anthony looks her dead in the eyes. "That's exactly the point. The only question is… whose baby will it be?" He shrugs. "And that's what makes it so fun."

"This is ridiculous," Camilla says. "You never said anything about a baby."

"We said everything about your body being ours in any way whatsoever … in exchange for fifty million dollars. Are you sure you want to be here?" Anthony asks her.

She balls her fists but doesn't say another word.

"Good." He gives us a lopsided smile. "Now … let's see who's going to go first."

Devon grins as he spins the wheel and bites his lip as he looks at each of the girls, probably wondering which position he's going to fuck us first. It makes me wonder if he's already forgotten about Lauren so quickly.

I watch in silence as the wheel slowly comes to a stop with the arrow pointing at my picture.

211

Everyone looks at me like I should know what to do.

Max steps forward. "Naomi, strip."

I glare at him before reaching for my zipper at the side of my body and pulling it down. My dress peels away, and I step out of my heels to rid myself of the dress. My bra comes off next, and as the clasps unhook and the straps fall off my shoulders, Devon's tongue dips out to slowly lick his lips again.

My face is completely blank as it drops to the ground while Anthony's pants begin to tent.

As I proceed to take off my panties, the girls behind me look at me with pity. I don't even have to see them to feel their gaze like lasers in my back.

When I'm naked, and my nipples are hardened from the cold, all three men have hard-ons.

Max holds out his hand, and I take it. He guides me to the bench and helps me lie down. One by one, he slides my legs apart and shackles my ankles to the wood. As I lie now, I can't keep my head up, which tilts over the edge of the bench.

I'm open and wide. Exactly how they want me.

Max towers above me. "Good girl," he says, gently caressing my cheek.

"The rest of you will sit down and watch," Anthony muses as he unbuttons his shirt. "Pick a seat."

The girls scramble to find a place to sit while I lie here, cold and uncomfortable, waiting for the ordeal to start. I take comfort in the fact that one of them will lie here next and that they will cycle through us all until it's finished. At least I get to go first and won't be a sloppy second.

Devon kicks off his shoes as Anthony throws his shirt

in the corner. Meanwhile, Max has already taken off his tie and blue shirt and dropped them to the floor. He's now unzipping his pants and taking off his shoes. The moment the men reveal their hard-on to the girls, more gasps are audible, and when I look at Latisha and how she's licking her lips and blinking fast, I just know she's dying to go next.

Maybe I should recommend her.

I laugh to myself as the now naked men step forward and position themselves near the bench.

"Do you have any questions before we start?" Max asks.

I close my eyes and shake my head. "I'm ready for whatever comes next."

"Ha-ha ... cum ..." Devon snorts.

No one thinks he's funny except him.

Then he asks, "Who's going to take her pussy first?"

"Well, since I'm already between her legs," Anthony muses as he claims his spot, "I am."

I feel like a piece of meat bartered to the highest bidder. What a fuck show.

"Fine," Devon growls, and he settles for my hand instead.

"Now, Naomi ... you do understand that it's your job to make us come?" Max asks, and he winks as he looks down at me. I'm sure that wink means something, and I bet I know what. It has something to do with the fact that he wants to come inside me ... and that if we want to win together, we need to make sure he's the one who comes inside my pussy.

I nod, preparing for what's to come by breathing in and out slowly.

"Let's begin," Max says, and he presses a timer

positioned on a small table behind him.

His brothers move toward me and start rubbing themselves until they're fully hard. Then they place their members on my skin. First is Devon, who grabs my hand and wraps it around his cock.

"Stroke me," he says.

I do what he asks, but only because I must.

Anthony's dick swiveling back and forth across my pussy distracts me, and for a moment, I wonder if I should say something about the fact that I'll never get wet for him.

Apparently, he's already thought of that because he immediately grabs a bottle of lube from another cabinet to the left and smears it all over his cock and me.

"You have such a nicely shaven pussy," he murmurs. "Makes me wanna come all over it."

He slips his cock between my folds like he's preparing it … or me.

I try to ignore him as I focus on Max who's been jerking off above me. He hovers closer and lets the tip rest on my lips. My mouth opens instinctively. He slides inside with ease. I'm so used to his taste that it already makes me horny just from having him on my tongue.

Suddenly, Anthony slams into me, and I suck in a breath … right when Max thrusts in his cock.

I almost choke and gurgle from the feel of him down my throat as Anthony buries himself into me deeply.

Max slaps my left cheek. "Focus, Naomi," he growls.

I wonder whether he means on him or on Anthony.

I don't want Anthony to come inside me, so I have to avoid it at all cost.

Relax my muscles and don't clamp up. Let him fuck me

all I want, I don't care. Or at least, that's what I tell myself.

Devon suddenly pinches my nipple, making me squeal against Max's cock.

"Keep jerking me off," Devon says.

I try to work him as well as I can, as I'd love for him to come on my stomach instead of in my pussy. Anything but that. However, he doesn't seem remotely close to busting his nut.

Anthony thrusts faster, and I feel my pussy thump from arousal. Fuck. It feels so wrong. Being fucked from all three angles by three guys while all the girls are watching. It's like a sex scene but kinkier. And I'm not even sure I mind it that much.

Max takes his cock and rubs my saliva all over his length before sliding back in again. He holds my face while he does it—gently, not roughly. I don't even mind it that much. It keeps my mind off the fact that Anthony is claiming my pussy as if it belongs to him when it doesn't. In my head, I imagine it's a dildo going in. The only one I can't replace is Devon's cock in my hand.

The alarm clock going off makes me jolt, and Max pulls his cock from my throat. "Damn, I was enjoying that a little too much." The head of his length bobs up and down, and it makes me smile. Fuck me. I shouldn't be happy that he liked it so much.

Anthony presses his fingers to his lips and places them on my clit. "This tight pussy almost made me come," he murmurs before walking away.

My lip twitches as he approaches my face, and Max steps aside. All the men switch places now, and Devon positions himself between my legs. I close my eyes as

Anthony lingers over my face, the reminder of him throat fucking me already making me gag before he even starts.

Max's gentle hand as he guides me to his dick makes me a little bit more comfortable. Until Anthony starts the timer.

"Time to fuck," Anthony muses, and he immediately grabs my neck and slides his dick into my mouth.

I don't even have the time to say anything. All I can feel is a dick in my throat, making me lose my breath, and a dick in my hand, stiffening with each rub. I picture fucking Max and Max alone. With my eyes closed, it's much easier to forget that the other two are even here. In my head, the girls don't even exist, and this contract is solely based on my relationship with Max. No matter how rocky it has been, it's the only constant in this house.

Devon enters my pussy like he already owns it, fucking me raw within seconds. He's like a beast smashing against me, his fingers digging into my leg as he goes about his way.

I try to concentrate on the sound of Max's moans as I touch the base of his length, hoping the timer will go off soon.

"Look at me," Anthony commands.

When I don't open my eyes, he slaps my cheek. "Obey me."

I do what he asks, but only because I know what happens when he gets mad.

The look in his eyes is full of lust, and it makes me want to bite down.

After gazing at me, he smears my saliva all over my face and then forces my head down, only to dive in with his cock. His hands lock tightly around my neck, making it even harder to accept him.

Every damn time, I can barely breathe. It's nerve-wracking, but at the same time, knowing that I'm close to Max calms me down a bit. At least he's here to watch over me, and I know he'll stop this whole scene if he only thinks for one moment that his brother is hurting me.

The tip of his cock bounces in my throat, and I swallow to keep my composure. I'm not going to have a meltdown here on this table. Not now when I've already gotten this far.

"Fuck me; your throat is so wide. How am I supposed to resist?" Anthony growls.

"You know what you're supposed to do," Max replies.

"Shut up." Anthony keeps fucking me, and somehow, at the same time, Max's dick grows harder in my hand. Maybe it's because I'm squeezing.

"Fuck …" Anthony moans, and his dick tenses in my throat.

His balls slap against my face, the smell bringing back memories of that time with Britt in his room. I close my eyes as I feel him thrust into my throat, trying to ignore the pounding going on in my pussy, but it's impossible. My senses are being attacked from all sides, and it's useless to fight the arousal.

Suddenly, a thick stream of cum spurts into the back of my throat, and I cough and swallow to get it to go down.

"Fuck … swallow it all," Anthony groans, pushing in until his base rests against my lips.

I gag on his cum which still seeps down.

The timer goes off in the middle of it all.

Max immediately slides away from my hand as Anthony slowly pulls his flaccid length from my throat, and I gasp for air.

Max pushes aside Devon, who wasn't even done impaling me, but is forcefully removed.

"My turn," Max chews.

"Geez, you don't have to be a dick about it," Devon says.

Max ignores him and looks me directly in the eye as he positions himself between my legs and grabs my thighs, almost as if he's telling me that he's coming for me.

Anthony moves to my hand, and I breathe a sigh of relief, only to come face to face with Devon ... the monster who killed Lauren.

"Don't worry, babe. I'm going to give you everything my brothers couldn't give you," Devon says with a smirk on his face as his cock lingers near my mouth.

"Stick out your tongue," he says.

I do what he asks, and then I taste myself on his dick.

"Sweet, huh? Just like your pussy," he says with a grin.

If I wasn't tied to this bench, I'd smack his head against it.

"Let's continue," Max says, cocking his head at Devon.

"Yeah, yeah ..." Devon pushes the timer, and the men begin again.

Max slowly circles around my pussy, his dick pulsing against my skin. I focus on him and him alone, even though Anthony settles near my hand and forces me to jerk off his half-hard dick.

The moment I feel Max enter me, I am lost. Lost to desire. Lost to his control.

I can feel it inside me, from the way he fucks me to the way he grasps my legs and holds me down. He owns my body ... and we both know it.

With him inside me, I can completely ignore Anthony. And even Devon, who forcefully enters my throat so fast I can't even breathe. But it doesn't matter. Everything ceases to exist as long as I can feel Max pumping inside me. His rhythm is soothing. Always the same pace. Predictable. It pulls me through the ordeal and even makes my blood rush down.

His thumb circles my clit as he growls, "I want you to come when I do. Can you do that for me?"

"Yes," I murmur as Devon allows me to breathe but only for a second.

"My brother's so nice to you, isn't he?" Devon muses, which I ignore.

"Focus on me," Max says.

I listen to him and his moans, his thrusts, his grip on my body. I zone out to the point of not even giving a shit that Devon is fucking my throat like a madman while he groans like a beast. Not even when he sinks into me until the base and makes me gag ... and comes.

His seed jets onto the back of my tongue, and I'm forced to swallow as he's still inside me. Then he takes his cock out, still spurting away, and he covers my face and breasts with cum. All while Max is thrusting so fast, I feel like I'm about to explode. The sensations are too much for me to handle.

"Come, now!" Max growls.

It only takes his voice for me to fall apart.

My body convulses, sweet bliss rushing over me, and Max's length thrusting into me a final time, pulsing as he ejaculates. His groan makes it that much raunchier, and the way he pushes in and out again to push his seed in only makes me want to come again.

I'm out of breath, and my red-hot, sweaty body is covered in man juices.

Jesus fucking Christ.

I don't think I've ever been fucked this hard.

Anthony grins as he looks at my wet, naked body, and says, "Next."

21

Accompanying Song: "Dark Star" by Jaymes Young

MAX

At night

Once I claimed Naomi's pussy, there was nothing left to fight for.

She was unshackled, helped off the table, and told to put her clothes on again.

Then the wheel was spun again. Another girl was chosen. And so began the entire process anew.

This time, however, it was different. After Naomi had left the room with her clothes in her hand, with all the women watching her stature as she walked off with her pride still intact, there was a clear change.

The mood ... the temperature ... the air.

It shifted toward something more sinister. Something

dark.

It's like they collectively decided they could overcome this game.

Just because of her.

The first girl to go after Naomi was Latisha, who was all too keen on getting up on the bench. She seemed a little too excited, and it bothered me, especially when she so vehemently insisted that Anthony would come in her pussy. I guess she really was head-over-heels with him. Or at least, with the idea of being married to him and having his baby.

Some girls do whatever it takes to get the one they want. She seemed like one of them, and I didn't want anything to do with it, so I was happy when her turn finally ended, even though Anthony won the round.

The next girl picked was Britt, and she went up the bench so quietly you could hear a pin drop. It was magnificent. And even though she cried, she didn't utter a word.

The only thing that struck me as odd was the fact that once she was shackled, one girl had her hand in the air. Stacey.

She asked if she could join us. If it would be allowed. Maybe she could be of use. After all ... we wanted to fuck all the girls this day. Why wait and do them one by one?

So Anthony invited her up because he liked the idea of fucking two beautiful women at the same time.

But he far more enjoyed the idea of them playing with each other.

I admit, I'm a sucker for the kinky side of life at times, and when I saw her take off her clothes and join us, I did regain my appetite. However, it was because my brother invited her that she was allowed to come up. I would never have agreed on my own.

Still, Stacey positioned herself above Britt, sixty-nine.

And Anthony and Devon made them lick each other.

While they fucked her ass.

At times, Britt was commanded to lick Anthony's balls while he fucked Stacey in the pussy.

And other times, Devon would stick his thumb and index finger in Stacey's ass and pussy while he fucked Britt's mouth. Stacey even licked the cum off Britt's pussy when Devon was done with her. It was a fucking orgy beyond my imagination.

But still, I missed Naomi.

I didn't care to fuck the others as much as I did her. I was spent already.

I admit I practically gave the girls to my brothers. They could go on for hours and still have a hard-on. I could only do that if Naomi was there, but she had already completed her task.

I grab my whiskey and stare at the fire ahead, the crackling flames reminding me of how some girls tried to do their best to seduce us into picking them. Dancing naked. Stripping seductively. Offering themselves as the next willing victim.

But their efforts are all in vain.

I have my eyes on one thing alone, and nothing will stop me from reaching my goal, no matter how much pussy is thrown at my face.

***

Naomi

Day 19

Everyone's losing their mind.

It's not me, it's them.

The girls ... I've never seen so many of them come unhinged at the same time.

Latisha's been offering herself to the men every single hour of the day, practically begging them to fuck her as she follows them around like a weak lamb. Camilla has resorted to helping the cooks in the kitchen, preparing her favorite meals, which she keeps serving to the men and herself on top of that.

Jordan's buried herself in a mountain of books, and she doesn't speak. Literally, she hasn't opened her mouth since the last game. Honestly, I can't even remember what her voice sounds like.

And then there's Stacey and Britt, who've been using oils and ointments and perfume to spray and massage each other until everyone can smell them from miles away. They're even taking baths together, pouring in so much sparkly salt their bodies glimmer when they come out.

And me? I spend half the time staring out into nothingness on the balcony and watching the news on the television, wondering if anyone's missing me yet.

But now, I've settled for reading a book in the bath. The girls are all out with Anthony, checking out his garden as he apparently also grows many flowers in the backyard. It's not for me, and I couldn't care less about wooing him. I've already found my match.

When the water is up to the right point, I close the faucet and take off my bathrobe, stepping in to soak in the warm water. I close my eyes for a few minutes before grabbing my book and turning around to read. I think I sit there for a good half hour before the water cools to lukewarm.

Suddenly, I hear a noise from behind the door.

Two girls are chatting as they enter the room.

I thought I wasn't going to have any company until after a good two hours had passed. That's what Anthony said anyway, but maybe some girls were tired of him. I can imagine.

However, I don't like not being alone in here, so I quickly get out and pull the plug on the water.

"I don't understand. Nothing I do works." It sounds like Britt.

"Oh, honey … it's okay." Stacey's comforting her.

I put on my robe and listen to their conversation, leaning close against the door.

"He just doesn't seem interested in me."

I wonder if she means Anthony because last I recall, he fucked her up pretty good.

"Max already has his eyes set on Naomi. You know that."

My heart skips a beat.

"I know … I just don't think I could settle for any of the other guys. They scare me."

"Me too." I hear them huddle up on the bed, but I don't know where they are or what they're doing. I just hear the muffled sounds.

"You know you don't have to like one of them. I mean we only have to get pregnant."

"That only scares me more," Britt says, whimpering a little.

"Oh, girl … c'mere. I know what you're feeling."

"Really?"

"Yeah … I have the same problem. I don't like any of them. I don't want to be here, but I have no choice. I have to pay off my loans, and I need this money more than anything."

Huh. If she only knew these brothers were the cause of all her misery.

"It's going to be okay," Stacey says. "We'll make it. You'll see."

"At least, I have you …" Britt mumbles.

"Yes … you always have me. I will be here, no matter what. I don't care what happens. You and me pull through, got it?" Stacey's voice is soft.

So soft, I can't even hear what they're saying next.

So I quietly turn the handle on the door and open it.

Only to find them kissing.

In shock, my jaw drops, and so does my hand as it slips from the door, which swooshes open. The girls notice me, their lips still partially locked as they gaze my way.

Terror floods their eyes.

"Na-Naomi …" Britt murmurs.

226

"Oh, god," Stacey says as she pulls away from Britt, her eyes solely focused on me. "Naomi. I didn't know you were here."

"Yeah," I say, narrowing my eyes. "This is the women's bedroom. Where else would I be?"

"I thought everyone was out in the yard."

I fold my arms. "I thought you were too."

"We were ... for a little while ... but Anthony went inside, and he told us everyone could do what they wanted. I guess the other girls stayed outside," Britt mumbles as she gazes down at the bed.

"Please don't say anything," Stacey suddenly says. "Please."

I cock my head at the sound of her begging.

I like it.

"Please. I know what it looked like," she says.

It looked like I finally uncovered the truth. Those girls never liked the men. They only liked each other.

"We just needed each other for a moment. That's all," she utters, swallowing, visibly shaken.

I lick my lips and watch them quiver in place, wondering what happens next. I'm not the one to decide.

"Yeah, please don't tell the guys," Britt pleads. "They'll hurt us."

I smash my lips together and turn around because I just remembered I left my earrings in the bathroom. As I walk through the door, Stacey says, "Say something."

"What's there to say?" I reply, without looking back.

"You won't tell a soul, right?"

I don't answer. I just grab my earrings and put them back in my ears. The girls are still staring at me, their hands

227

still locked together like they'll stand together against me if they have to. Like they'd be prepared to kill.

I smile, but that smile turns into laughter instead.

"What's so funny?"

Like either of them would ever be remotely capable of such an act.

No.

Only two women in this house would kill for this game, and it's neither of them.

I cock my head and squint as the girls shake their heads, like deer in headlights. They don't know what's coming, but I do.

I slowly lift my finger at the top left corner of this room and point at the camera aimed straight at them.

Their jaws come undone.

And I can't help but feel invigorated.

Now, their chances of winning are as good as over, which means more chances for me. It's an eat or get eaten world, and I'm at the top of the food chain.

Is it wrong? Hell, yes. Do I care? Not in my fucking lifetime.

**

MAX

Accompanying Song: "Medieval Warfare" by Grimes

"Oh, my fucking god," Devon yells, as he scoots back

his chair, his hands ruffling through his hair like he's seen a bad car crash on YouTube.

Anthony stands next to him, bent over with his palms flat on the desk, his muscles tense.

"What?" I ask, frowning as they never normally sit behind the laptop.

"They fucking kissed," Anthony growls.

My eyes widen as I step closer. "Who did?"

"Stacey and Britt."

I approach them from behind and glance at the screen over their shoulders. The guys are re-watching the scene over and over again, but all I can look at is Naomi who casually points at the camera like she's always known they were there. And the wicked smile on her face that follows.

"Fuck, we can't let them fucking get away with that," Devon growls as he pushes himself up. "I'm gonna get 'em."

"Why?" I turn as he goes to the door. "What do you want to do about it?"

"They fucking love each other? Not on my watch."

"Wait for me," Anthony says as he rushes after him.

I follow the two out the door and up the stairs. The closer they get, the bigger their steps, and I can almost feel the rage dripping off them. Devon is consumed by it. I just know it. Seeing those two girls kiss set him off.

"Devon, don't," I say, as he jerks the door open and slams it against the wall.

"If you're not on my side, stay out of it!" he screams in my face.

The girls inside the room look up, terrified, as they notice us enter.

229

"You two!" Devon screams at Stacey and Britt, who jump up from the bed. "C'mere. NOW!"

Britt shakes her head, tears running down her cheek, and Stacey blatantly says, "No."

Fuck.

She shouldn't have.

All it takes is one word. One fucking word for my brother to snap. And it just happened. That click ... it was visible; I could see it in his eyes.

"You think you can kiss each other in my house and get away with it? Huh?" he screams at them. "You think I wouldn't notice that you love each other more than you love *us*?"

"Stop," I yell as I grab Devon by the arms and try to hold him back.

"Fuck, no," Anthony says, and he jerks my arm away. "Those girls deserve punishment. Remember the fucking rules," he growls.

Before I know it, Devon's already up in the girl's faces.

From the side of his pants emerges a gun.

Bang.

That's all it takes.

One shot.

Stacey is gone.

A red hole in her forehead. Her body sinks to the floor. A loud scream ensues.

In shock, I stare at my brother and Britt, who's going ballistic, and Naomi who stands at the back with her hand over her mouth.

"Devon!" I scream.

"We told you we wanted full devotion. Love only us, no

one else. But you failed. And you know what? You sob too fucking much," Devon growls at Britt.

As fast as my legs can take me, I rush to him.

But not before he's reached into his other pocket, fished out a knife, and slit her throat.

Blood pours like a fountain from her neck, and it makes me stop in my tracks and sink to my knees.

Too late.

With my hands on my knees, palms up, I watch my brother tuck his knife back into his pocket and push her to the ground.

So many gasps coming from her dying body, it makes me want to choke.

In the distance, Naomi still stands frozen, but her eyes glaze with tears and unspoken words as she stares directly into my eyes.

Anthony casually walks past me, ripping a white sheet off Stacey's bed, and covers the bodies with it ... Right before the rest of the girls run in and come to a screeching halt in front of the door, probably alarmed from the gunshot and scream.

Their silence reminds me of the deafening sound of murder.

Part IV
The Culmination

22

Accompanying Song: "Are We Having A Party" by Cliff Martinez

Naomi

Day 20

Four brides left.

We're running thin.

I'm not sure if I should be elated or damn shocked. I mean the way they went wasn't exactly gentle. I watched the blood gush out of those girls like waterfalls. And all the guys did was just watch. None of them helped.

We're all sadistic fucks.

Just watching Devon kill them like it's no big deal.

Sometimes, I wonder if I even have a heart.

If I do, it must be pitch black in there.

Camilla, Latisha, Jordan, and I watched in silence as the baggers came to take Stacey and Britt away. The beds were stripped and all their belongings removed. They even cleaned the carpets until the stains were gone. If I didn't know any better, it's like they never even existed.

We sit in the women's bedroom, staring each other down like hawks. The men haven't shown their faces since yesterday, and I bet it's because they're either afraid, or they have to keep their temper in check so they don't kill more of us. Or maybe it's both of those. After all … they need us. And I think Devon forgot about that fact.

"How could this happen?" Jordan mutters out of nowhere.

"Easy. We weren't paying attention," Camilla says.

"She was," Latisha says, narrowing her eyes at me. "Why didn't you stop him?"

"Stop who?" I say.

"Devon."

I snort. "Like I could take a gun *and* a knife from his hand."

"I mean when he came in. You could've prevented that."

"It was already too late," I answer. "By the time I showed the girls the camera, the men were already bursting in."

"Right …" She makes a face and takes a deep breath. "Yet you just stood there with a gaping mouth as they laid there, dying."

"Excuse me?" I cock my head.

Is she trying to pin it on me? Get the girls to hate me?

"Latisha …" Camilla sighs.

234

"No, she needs to hear this." Latisha's fingers curl around the chair. "It's because of her that they're now dead."

"What? They were kissing. I didn't have anything to do with that," I retort. "If anything, they should've known that was what happens when you don't pay attention to the rules."

"Rules? The rules never stated you couldn't kiss each other," she growls.

"The rules stated that we were there for the guys. We are at their disposal. We are their pets. We are their lovers. They do not want us feeling any emotions whatsoever unless it's for them." I lean in, my fingers digging into my chair. "That's why they died. Because they were intimate with each other *without* the men present. Without it being *for* the guys."

"In any case, we're with four now, and there are three men. Little choice left," Jordan chimes in. "If they keep going at this rate, there won't be any left."

"Well … it's not like they can't find other girls to make their brides," Camilla says.

It's quiet for some time as everyone realizes they could just as well kill us all off.

But I'm not worried. Max wants me too much. He's infatuated with me. He'd never let the guys hurt me. Never.

At least, not more than they already have.

"They won't, right?" Latisha says. "I mean … I'm not going to give up that easily. I'll follow every damn rule if I have to, but I'm not leaving this house until I've won." She laughs it off as if it's no big deal. "I'm gonna be married."

"The question is whose wife will you be?" Camilla replies, cocking her head.

"Anthony's, of course," Latisha says, almost spitting venom as she speaks. "He's *mine*."

The look in her eyes makes everyone stare at her for a moment.

"If he proposes to me, that is," she suddenly adds. Latisha shrugs, and the conversation grows quiet.

Not soon after, we're all called out of our room but not for a game. A few days ago, we all went to the doctor to have our blood taken and tested, and now, they've come back with the results. Anthony herds us to the room that has the pool table in it, where Max and Devon sit on the couch. Devon stares at his hands that rest in his lap while Max is busy with the mail. Max opens the letter that contains the information and licks his finger to turn the pages around.

"Results are in," he says.

Anthony sits down in a chair to the left and casually pours himself a scotch.

"I know you're probably wondering why we made you do a blood test," Max says.

Jordan nods softly.

"It's because we wanna know if you're pregnant or not," Anthony muses, taking a sip. "Obviously, if you are, that's great. If you're not … well, then we gotta keep on fucking you until you are."

"What do you mean?"

"It means," Max intervenes, "that we want babies."

"Like we told you before," Devon adds. "We can do anything we want to your bodies as long as the contract lasts."

"And you want heirs …" Jordan mutters, her shoulders slumping.

"Exactly." Anthony winks, and it makes the hairs on the back of my neck stand up.

"Anyway, let's continue." Max clears his throat. "Camilla ..." He briefly glances at her. "Not pregnant."

She bites her lip and chews on the inside of her cheek as she folds her arms, not even caring to respond.

"Latisha ... not pregnant," Max continues.

"Dammit ..." Latisha mumbles.

"Naomi ... *not* pregnant." The way he pronounces each syllable as low as he can makes me want to grab the vase in the corner and smash it to bits.

When he reaches the end of the page, his eyes wander off for a second, and he turns the page a few times, checking if what he sees is correct. But then he opens his mouth. "Jordan. Pregnant."

I stare at her and so do the others. No one speaks a word. Except her.

"What?" she mumbles.

"Wait, whose is it?" Devon tries to snag the paper from Max's hand, but he won't let him. Everyone's eyes are on Max now, and the seconds that pass feel like ages.

He purses his lips and frowns, almost like he's confused. "It's Anthony's."

Everyone's jaw drops and Anthony's eyes widen. Jordan shakes her head, mumbling, "No..."

Anthony jumps up from his seat with a victory pose. "Fuck, yeah!"

He walks over to her and grabs her by the waist, twirling her around in his arm like she's suddenly become his favorite. "That's my girl!"

"Wait ..." she mumbles. "No ..."

"Yes, Jordan." He grabs her chin and forces her to look at him. "I've gotten you pregnant. You're *mine* now."

He smashes his lips onto hers, kissing her, even though she tries to push him away.

"Jesus, calm down, will ya …" Devon muses. "Take it to another room. I don't want to see you two get it on. I've seen enough dick for a while."

Jordan finally manages to push Anthony away, but not before he's stolen another kiss. His eyes are still on her like a tiger who's finally found his mate. And I'm horrified. Utterly fucking horrified. Because now, there's one less bachelor … and still, three girls who are potential threats.

I swallow away my pride and say, "Okay. Are we done here?"

"Yes. That was all," Max replies.

I turn around and leave. I don't care whether they make more babies or whether Anthony proclaims her as his chosen bride. I just want to be alone.

Camilla and Latisha follow suit, but not before Latisha throws a temper tantrum.

"You were supposed to pick me!" she yells. "Me! I wanted to be the one to give you everything." She cries like a baby as she storms around and leaves.

Luckily, she doesn't follow us into the women's bedroom. I don't know where she goes, but as long as she's not here, I'm happy. I can't deal with her crazy ass right now.

I sit down on my bed and grab my purse, checking myself in the mirror. I'm a freaking mess.

"Well … that went great," Camilla says, throwing herself on the couch.

"I really don't feel like talking right now," I say.

"Well, excuse me." She sighs.

"It's not you, it's me," I say, smiling at her. She returns a petty smile, which only makes me smile harder.

"Don't take me as a fool, Naomi. I know what's going on here."

"I don't think you're a fool, Camilla," I reply. "Tell me what's going on."

"Three girls left without a man … and only two bachelors. Someone's going to end up with that motherfucker who killed Lauren, and it isn't going to be me."

I suppose that's a veiled threat, so I don't respond.

"And you know … those men aren't just seeking brides and making babies," she says. "They're making heirs. And that can only mean one thing … someone's gonna take over the company."

"So?"

She frowns. "It means only one of *them* can win. Those brothers … only *one* of them will be in charge. They can't all three be in charge. It doesn't work like that."

"Hmm … interesting," I muse, pretending that I didn't already know that.

"And I think I already know who it's going to be …"

"Really? And who's that?"

"Well, it isn't Anthony," she says, slamming her lips together like she wants to say more but doesn't. She knows damn well it's information she could use to her advantage. Clever girl.

"You can say what you want, but Jordan is pregnant," I say. "So they're gonna win."

"I'm not so sure. How do we know Max was speaking the truth? For all we know, he could be lying to our faces to make his own move." She eyes me like she knows he's into me and no one else.

I shrug. "Whatever. We'll find out soon enough."

"I guess you're right," she muses, like she's not at all on edge, even though I know she is. I can tell from her rigid posture.

"Why did you come back?" I ask.

She sighs. "I don't even know, to be honest."

"Yeah, you do," I reply.

She throws a piercing glare at me.

"Money," I say softly. "And ... because they told you you had no other choice."

"How do you know?" she frowns.

"They did the same thing to me ..." I cock my head. "What else do you know?"

"That I was threatened? They'd kill me unless I came back here? What else am I supposed to know that you don't?"

Interesting.

I purse my lips and mull it over.

"But you know you can't win this either ... are you afraid they'll kill you afterward?"

She just stares without giving me a hint of emotion.

"No?" I ask. "Or do you think you can still win one of their hearts?"

"I don't need to give you an explanation," she hisses. "You think I'm only here for myself, that I'm like you, but I'm not. I care about the girls in here. I worry about them. I don't want to see them hurt."

240

"You care about them?" I scoff. "No wonder you left."

"These men are insane. If they even threatened to kill me, what would they do to *them*? The girls who I left behind? If they were smart, they would've packed their bags and ran with me!" she yells.

"Why do you care about them? You barely know them."

"I'm not a monster!" Her eyes fill with tears. "I care about people. I don't need to know anyone to care about them."

"Right ..." I sigh. "But they stayed because of the money," I reply. "And you know that."

She shrugs it off like it's the truth. Like she'd jump in front of a train for these women. I can't believe that simply because I don't feel the same way. But she's always struck me as the mother hen type.

It's quiet for some time before she breaks the silence.

"All I know is that someone is pregnant. And that someone isn't you," she says, throwing me another glare.

Just that single word ... pregnant ... can make the hairs on the back of my neck stand up. Why? Because she's right. It isn't me ... when it should have been.

We both know this conversation has ended, so I get up from the bed and clear my throat. "I'm going to take a stroll."

"Have fun," she answers, and she immediately gets up to make some coffee.

I walk through the door and take a few breaths, shaking my head at the thought that Anthony would take the company for himself and ruin my plans.

I don't go outside. I go straight to Max's room.

23

Accompanying Song: "Only Human" by Cold Showers

MAX

She storms into my room and slams the door shut behind her then starts to pace around.

"What a nice surprise …" I murmur.

"Shut up," she mutters.

"Hello to you too." I sit down on my bed and lean back, watching her body move fluidly through my room like a fire spreading fast.

She looks at me through the corner of her eye. "Did you threaten Camilla to come back?"

"My brother did," I answer.

"And Hyun?"

"No."

"Don't lie to me," she hisses, clearly upset.

"I'm not. They don't like her, and neither do I."

"Your brother had a thing for her. I remember that," she says, still pacing.

"They're not interested anymore. They already had their favorites."

"Then why Camilla?" she whisper-yells.

"Because she wasn't weak, and my brother wanted another option. That's all."

"Weak? So that's what this is about," she mumbles, almost like she's talking to herself.

"Are you just going to pace around my room or are you going to sit down?" I pat the bed.

She briefly glances at me but doesn't take me up on my offer. "Suit yourself," I say, shrugging. "I know you're not here to talk about Hyun. Or Camilla. I do know why you're *really* here."

She stops in her tracks.

"The pregnancy test," I say.

Her eyes are on me like a hawk as she licks her lips, her nostrils flaring. "Is it true? Is she really pregnant with his baby?"

"Yes."

The news hit me as hard as it did her.

I admit it was arrogant to assume my plan would work without fault. I was a bit careless in my effort to drug my brothers. Maybe I didn't give them the right consistency. Or maybe his sperm was just so goddamn thick, just like his head.

"Goddammit ..." Naomi rubs her forehead.

"Are you jealous?" I jest.

"Fuck yes, I'm jealous. I want to win," she retorts, and I love her honesty. "Tell me she isn't pregnant. Tell me it's all a lie."

"It's not. Why do you think I'm lying?"

"You'd have every reason to do so …"

"True," I say, nodding. "But I wasn't lying."

She narrows her eyes at me. "Why not?"

"They would've found out anyway, regardless of whether or not I told the truth when I read that paper out loud. My brothers would've snatched it right out of my hand if I lied and said it was you who was pregnant."

She breathes out a hard breath through her mouth and purses her lips. "You know as well as I do that this could be a game changer."

"Yes …" I entwine my hands and stare at them.

She stares me down. "If she *is* truly pregnant and manages to actually give birth, he will win the company. Correct?"

I cock my head and mull it over for a second. I hate saying the truth out loud like that. It gives her too much ammunition. However, she seems to have figured everything out already, so denying the truth is silly and won't get me anywhere with her.

So I nod slowly.

"What are you going to do about it?" she asks, her fingers sliding along my cabinet, resting briefly atop a letter-opener before she continues her stride.

A lopsided smile forms on my lips as I squint and say, "Are you suggesting something, Naomi?"

She raises her brows innocently. "I'm not suggesting anything."

"I know what you're thinking. But is that really an option?" I tap my fingers against each other.

"You tell me," she muses.

"I'll tell you what I think. I think my brother is going to keep her locked in his room and guard her twenty-four-seven. You're asking the wrong question. The real question is what are *you* going to do about it?" My tongue dips out to lick my lips.

My words strike a chord with her because she takes one step back and picks up the letter-opener. Holding it loosely in her hand, she treads toward me, her red gown trailing behind her as elegantly as she is. Quietly menacing ... dangerously seductive. Perfect for me.

I look up as she stops in front of me and crawls on top of me, her knees beside my body, forcing me to lie down. She shows me the blade, holding it close to my throat.

"I could kill you right now," she whispers. "For ruining my life."

The metal strokes my neck, softly grazing my skin, and I feel a warm droplet running down.

"You could," I murmur into her ear. "Or you could spread your legs and let me fuck you."

She chuckles near my ear, licking the rim. "And why would I do that?"

Her tongue drags all the way down my neck, sucking up the little droplet of blood she created. My body instinctively bucks to meet hers, my cock already hard from her aggressive advances.

My fingers find their way under her gown, and I slide aside her panties to touch her pussy.

"Because that's what you really want. You want to win," I say, pulling her so close the blade almost pierces my skin. "You need this. Me. A baby." I lift my head, even though the letter-opener is still in my way, but she moves back with me, not allowing herself to cut me again. "You don't want to kill me. You *like* me … you love what I do to you. You enjoy this sadistic game as much as I do." I flick her clit, and her lips tremble as she feels me take control. "You're here to fuck. So let's fuck."

The letter-opener drops from her hand as my fingers entangle with hers, and her lips smash onto mine. I immediately roll her over and pin her wrists above her head, kissing her with fervor. She came into my room with a purpose. A goal. And I'm all about letting her win.

"Only one way you can win, Naomi … and that's to have my fucking baby."

"Only if she loses hers," she mutters between kisses.

"It'll fucking happen, trust me. I know my fucking brother." I shove her dress up, squeezing her ass tight. "Now shut up and let me fuck your brains out."

Growling like a fucking bear, I lean up and yank my belt out of the loops. "Take off your gown."

She complies, pulling it off sensually, even though I'm doing anything but going slow on her today.

"Turn around," I say with a dark voice, and she does exactly that. "Wrists on your back."

I tie the belt around her arms and make sure it's tight enough so she can't escape.

"Think I'm going to run?" she muses.

"No. I just don't want you to move while I fuck your body raw," I say with a smirk.

Then I push her down, her head flopping onto my bed. My fingers curl around her panties near her pussy, and I tear them off at the seam.

"Those were expensive," she says.

"I'll buy you three hundred more," I growl. "Now, spread your legs so I can give you what you came for."

"What I came for?" she retorts.

I rip down my zipper and unbutton my pants, and as my hard-on flips out of my boxer shorts, I say, "My cock."

I position myself behind her and fondle her pussy, which is already wet as fuck. "Horny?" I muse.

"Fuck you ..." she spits.

"You're only saying that because you hate that you love it so much." I smack her ass, which makes her squeal. "That's it. Make those sounds. It only gets me going."

I stick my finger into her pussy and then another, swirling around inside her. She moans out loud, her body tensing and relaxing again and again.

"Don't resist the need, Naomi," I say.

I pull out my fingers and bring them to her mouth. "Taste yourself."

When she parts her lips, I slide my fingers onto her tongue, making her taste herself. And right when she does, I shove my cock into her. Her moan makes me greedy, selfish, and I thrust in and out of her without holding back.

"That's it. Let me fuck that pussy like it needs to be fucked," I growl, holding each side of her ass like they're handles. I smack her again for a little extra oomph, the redness that follows spiking my arousal.

"You're an ass," she hisses.

"I know ... and you know what else? I'm going to fuck yours too."

I grin when I pull back out again and see her lips part and her eyes widen. I step off the bed, open the drawer, and take out the lube I had stashed there. Getting back on the bed, I squish it out above her ass, rubbing it in.

"What are you doing? That won't make me pregnant," she says.

"It won't, but I'm not coming in your ass. I'm just claiming my territory," I say with a lopsided grin as I watch her face contort.

"I never said—"

My cock going into her asshole interrupts her words.

God, I love that sound she makes. The gasp that just keeps on giving. Just like her body.

"Fuck, you're so fucking tight," I say, smacking her ass again as I plunge into her. I grab the belt wrapped around her wrists and hold it as a rein so I can fuck her harder.

"Sometimes, I really want to kill you," she huffs.

I laugh. "I'm going to be doing this a lot when you're my wife so get fucking used to it," I growl, and I stuff my finger into her pussy. "You belong to me, and you know it."

"Damn you and your fucking cock," she growls.

It only makes me thrust harder. "This fucking cock is going to make you come, so be happy."

With my index finger and thumb, I circle her clit and rub it between my fingers, making her knees weak. "See? Admit it. You like being mine." When she doesn't say a word, I smack her ass and growl. "Say it."

"Yes, I like it!" she screams, her body bouncing up and down from my thrusting.

I grin and lick my lips, feeling victorious in my mission to conquer her. "Finally."

***

Naomi

He twists my body into knots, and I like it.

He fucks me like I'm a blow-up doll, and I like it.

He claims control like some animal, and I like it.

Goddammit, I like everything. And I hate it.

I hate that I like him so much I couldn't even kill him when I had the chance.

I don't fucking want to. The only thing I want is for him to fuck my brains out, just like he said.

So when he twirls my clit and rams his cock into my ass, all I can do is moan and sigh, even though I can't do a thing to stop it. I'm powerless against him, and I hate being fucking powerless … but with him, it's a fucking drug.

A turn-on so powerful, it makes me want to beg.

"Fuck," I mutter into the sheets, feeling heady from his touch.

"Already there?" he muses. "Don't come yet." He pulls out of me and slaps my ass a final time, which makes me roll over. I can't help it; my hands are tied to my back. There's nothing I can do. Nothing, and it's so fucking intoxicating, I'm completely wet for him.

He pulls my leg up and lays it against his shoulder, scissoring me, his dick at the entrance to my pussy. As he pushes in, he grabs my breast and squeezes.

"Mine. All fucking mine." He thrusts and thrusts so hard, I can barely breathe.

With his fingers, he twists my nipple. "Say you're fucking mine!" he growls.

"I'm yours," I reply, and even though I despise myself for saying it, it's the truth.

"Damn right, you're mine." He sounds like an animal, the way he gruffly speaks and groans as he slams into me. "I'm going to fill you up to the brim with my cum. You ready for it?"

"Yes," I moan, as his fingers move from my breast to my clit, where he rubs me to the point that I'm about to come.

"Fuck …" I whisper.

"Yes. Come, Naomi. Let me see how ready this body is to receive my cum."

As he fondles me, the tip of his length grazes my G-spot, and I explode. All. Over. Him. I can feel it, and I gasp for air as my body trembles beneath him.

"Fuck, yes," he growls.

Four more thrusts and I feel him release, cum jetting into me, again and again. It just keeps coming, like a warm stream, filling me completely. And he keeps thrusting; not wanting to spill any of it, he continues to push it farther into me.

When he's done, he pulls out and slowly lowers my leg. After untying me, he grabs my face and pulls me up into a seated position. Still towering above me, he holds my cheek, and says, "You're not just mine because I can fuck you, Naomi. You're mine because I say you're mine"—he taps my chest—"in here. Your heart belongs to me, and you know it. Don't you dare deny it."

He leans in and presses a soft kiss to my lips, sealing the

deal. "We're too good together not to be," he whispers, kissing my doubts away. "You and me together. A wickedly twisted couple no one will be able to stand up to."

At this point, there is little to no point in fighting it any longer. My attraction to him is too strong. Too powerful to ignore. And I actually *want* him to kiss me, as crazy as it sounds.

Only one thing pulls me from his embrace.

A piercing scream ... and then a loud thud.

24

Accompanying Song: "Consummation" by Trent Reznor &
Atticus Ross

Naomi

I jolt up and out of bed, quickly throwing on a bathrobe that hangs from Max's closet, and then I rush out the door. However, before I can take three more steps, I come to a screeching halt.

In front of me is a body.

Half-naked and face down on the cold, hard floor.

Limbs twisted in ways I never thought possible.

Blood pouring from her nose and lips.

Jordan.

I scream and run toward her, kneeling near her body. Touching her body feels like touching pudding; blubbery. Her bones aren't just broken ... they're completely

252

shattered. She's wasted.

I place my finger on her neck to inspect for a pulse. It's barely there.

"Jordan? Fuck, say something," I whisper, trying to make sense of this.

Her blood-stained lips move, her eyes focusing on me as if she means to tell me something, but the words don't come out. All she does is gaze away ... and up, toward the balustrade.

I follow her gaze and find Camilla lunged over the balustrade near Anthony's room, staring at us in shock, her eyes teary. "Jordan!" she screams.

Her face is not just red from shock. She has a cut on her nose, blood seeping from the wound, and a definite bruise around her eye.

Suddenly, Anthony approaches her from the left, looking down at the body next to me ... His eyes widen as he realizes what happened. "Jordan? No!" he growls.

Then he looks at Camilla, who sees him too and turns to face him.

"You ..." Out of nowhere, Anthony pulls out a gun.

Within one second, he's shot Camilla.

Point-blank.

Dead between the eyes.

I scream and crawl away from the blood pooling underneath me. The bathrobe is already soaked in it.

"What the fuck happened?" Max yells as he comes out wearing only a pair of sweatpants. Then he spots Jordan's body. "Fuck, no."

"I don't know what happened," I say, sniffing, trying to wipe away the blood, and I smear it on the tiles. "She was already on the floor when I came out of the room."

He quickly checks her pulse. "She's gone."

I frown and feel her again. There's nothing left. With her last breath, she tried to show me what happened, but I still don't understand.

"You killed my baby!" Anthony screams at Camilla's body, stomping on her with his feet. "You killed my fucking baby, and now, I killed you!" he yells, still holding the gun out to her. "My baby. My wife. Gone!"

"Anthony!" Max runs off and up the stairs while I stay with the body. "Are you fucking insane?"

"You saw what happened!" Anthony spits back, his face red, slathered with tears. "She pushed her over!"

"You don't know that. None of us were here to see it," Max says as he approaches him, holding his hand up to stop Anthony from doing something he'll regret. "Maybe she jumped."

"NO!" Anthony screams, so loud it pierces my ears. "She would *never* do that to my baby."

I can't go up there. I can't witness how these two men bicker over dead corpses.

I can't comprehend how he just murdered a girl without even knowing what happened. Without even being there to witness the whole ordeal.

But then I spot something peculiar from the corner of my eye.

A hand disappearing behind a door leading to a bathroom upstairs.

I crawl up to my feet and back away from the bleeding body that was once Jordan. Without thinking, I go up the stairs, my ears still ringing from the sound of Jordan's scream. My hand leaves a bloody print on the railing as I take the last step up and into the hallway. Tentatively turning the handle, I take a breath and try to focus, even though the voices in my head tell me not to go in.

I do it anyway.

The bathroom is barely lit. I can tell this bathroom is hardly used. There are spiders in the top corners, cobwebs everywhere, and a certain smell hanging through the room. The stench of stagnant water ... mixed with old soap.

I push open the creaking door and see something move behind the curtain in the back of the room. I walk toward it, shivering from the sudden rush of cold sweeping over me. My fingers tremble as I clutch the curtain and slowly pull it back.

There, in front of a sink in the corner of the room, stands Latisha.

The water is running, and she's humming an eerie tune.

I don't say a word as I approach her and peek at her from the side to see her washing her hands.

For a second, I think I spot a drop of blood.

"I know you're watching me," Latisha says with a soft, outspoken voice.

"I'm not trying to hide," I reply, standing my ground.

She turns the handle of the faucet. "I'm so glad you're here now." Then she turns around. On her face too is the beginning of a bruise. "You make it so much easier."

I make a face. "You killed her, didn't you?"

Her face tightens, and she cocks her head. "Killed who?"

"You know who," I say without emotion.

A faint hint of a smile appears on her face. "Oh ... you

mean Jordan."

"You forced her to jump, but then how did you get the blood on your hand?" I mutter.

She clutches the sink and stares at me, bemused. "Go on."

"The bruise on your face indicates a fight. Camilla was there too. She saw you push Jordan. You two had a fight about it."

She turns her head to the other side, her smile growing bigger every second. "I love how smart you are ... how you see every, little detail."

"She knew what you were doing, and she tried to stop you. That's why you both have the bruises. That's why she has the cut on her face, and you're bleeding."

"Such a pity," she murmurs, taking a step in my direction.

I swallow away the lump in my throat. "But you threatened to kill her too. That's why she lost."

Latisha makes a gun symbol with her hand, presses it against her temple, and says, "Boom."

My nose twitches. "You set her up, so Anthony would kill her. Two birds with one stone." I frown. "Why her? Why Jordan?"

She shrugs. "I just wanted him. That's all."

"Anthony? This is about Anthony?"

"Of course, it's about Anthony. It's always been about him," she says, laughing a little like it's supposed to make sense. "I adore him. I worship him. And he needs to marry *me*." She puts her hand in her pocket and fishes out a knife. "And if you hadn't followed me, it would've turned out nicely for you."

I step back as she approaches me, holding out the knife in a threatening position.

"You could've lived happily ever after with Max, Naomi. All you had to do was ignore what you'd seen."

"I would've known, regardless," I reply.

"But at least you'd still be alive." She grins. "Now, you give me no choice but to kill you too."

"They'll know you did it," I say, walking in circles as she follows me around.

"I'll play the victim. Say you attacked me, and I defended myself."

"They'll never believe you," I hiss.

"Doesn't matter. There'd be only one of us left. They'll be the ones fighting over me, not the other way around."

"They didn't pick you. None of them did."

Her smile disappears instantly. "Shut up."

She lashes out, the knife inches away from my stomach. I lunge back, avoiding it narrowly.

She keeps slashing away, trying to cut me with it, not even stopping for a second to talk. The only way I have of avoiding her is by blocking the attack with a closet door. As she rams the knife into the wood, I use the opportunity to slam it into her so hard that it knocks her away, as well as the knife.

She comes at me in full force, giving me one blow to the face. But I quickly recuperate to punch her in the face, making her head tilt back. Then I grab her by the hair, twisting it and pulling it so hard she squeals. I ram her face down on the sink, making her bleed. A tooth falls to the floor.

Her screams fill me with excitement. A need so thrilling

it sets me on fire. A need to inflict pain.

However, she snatches a metal bottle of liquid soap and smashes it against my face so hard that I lose my balance and slip on the wet floor. But as I fall to the ground, she immediately comes at me. She wraps her fingers around my throat, choking me.

"You fucking bitch … you almost ruined my plan."

My eyes feel like they're about to pop from my head; that's how hard she squeezes the life out of me. I try to fight her off, clawing my way out of her grasp, but it's no use. My eyes skitter across the room to try to find something to use, and I spot something shiny on the floor so close to me I can almost reach it.

The knife.

She's suffocating me to the point I can't even speak. With my last bit of energy, I pick up the knife that she dropped, and I jam it into her stomach.

She releases me, and I take a long, hard gasp as she sinks to the floor beside me.

But the fight isn't over yet.

I pull the knife from her body and ram it between her ribs.

And then I do it again.

And again.

And again.

All while her eyes are searching for a way out.

Pleading for me to stop.

Her lips forming O's as the sounds of death escape her mouth.

But I don't stop.

Not until every inch of her skin is punctured. Until her

body is nothing but holes with filling.

Until I can see the realization in her eyes that she loses and I win.

Until my body is covered in her blood that sprayed out like a fountain of revenge.

Revenge for the girls she killed.

Or maybe a fountain of rage that finally spilled over.

Because damn … this fury flowing through my veins is powerful.

Once her eyes have turned gray, I stand up and pat down my dress. I walk to the sink and set the knife down, looking at my blood-painted skin with pride.

I don't even want to wash it off.

Clearing my throat, I throw my hair back over my shoulder and walk over her corpse, striding out the door.

25

Accompanying Song: "Scream" by Grimes ft. Aristophanes

MAX

I have to physically drag my brother away from Camilla before he finally stops smashing her. Her body is completely obliterated and unrecognizable to the point of it looking more like a sack of bones and blood than a human being.

"Let go of me!" Anthony screams in my face. "Fucking hell. All because I went to get a glass of water for her. And now she's fucking dead!"

I finally manage to snatch the gun from his hand, and I throw it over the balustrade.

"What the fuck happened here?" Devon yells from down below. "Jesus."

I look over the railing and see him pick up the arm of the lifeless body on the floor.

"Don't fucking touch her!" Anthony says, sticking up

his middle finger at his brother.

"Why not? She's dead anyway," Devon muses, dropping her floppy hand like a stone.

I shake my head and close my eyes.

But when I open them again, I spot Naomi walking out of the bathroom in the hallway up ahead … covered in blood.

My eyes widen, and I immediately run toward her. But then I hear my brother's rampaging scream.

"Max? Naomi? You …"

Before he can reach her, I wrap my arms around her and hold her close to me, protecting her from him as he comes charging at her.

"If you lay even one fucking finger on her, I'll put a bullet in your head," I growl.

His nostrils flare as his hands turn to fists. "What did you do?"

She gently points at the bathroom, insinuating we look.

My brother smashes the door open, and I look through it as he barges in and stares at Latisha's body.

"She pushed Jordan over the railing," Naomi says.

"How the fuck do we know you're speaking the truth?" Anthony growls. "For all we know, you could've killed her and then Latisha."

"She was with me the entire night," I say, looking her in the eyes to confirm. "She even found Jordan lying on the floor. No way could she have run upstairs, pushed her down, and then ran back downstairs again to pretend she never knew what happened, all in the span of twenty seconds. Because that's how long it took me to put on these sweatpants and walk out my room to see Jordan's body lying on the floor." I sigh. "So no, the answer is that Naomi didn't do anything. It was Latisha."

"Who's now conveniently dead," Devon muses.

"Shut up," I growl at him. "Where were you all this time anyway?"

"Listening to music with the headphones," he replies.

"I don't fucking care," Anthony spits. "Latisha's dead too now."

"Yes, and we'll worry about all that later." I turn around with Naomi in my arms, determined to keep at least her safe.

"What about my girl? My baby?" Anthony says, but luckily, he stays put as I go back down with her.

"We'll figure it out later. First, I gotta clean her up."

I quickly bring Naomi downstairs and into my bedroom then I lock the door. I grab her hand and pull her with me to the shower, which I turn on. Then I drape the stained bathrobe off her bloody body and make her get under the spray.

She doesn't move or say a word, and I wonder if she's silent because she knows anything she says now will either incriminate her or jeopardize her safety in this building.

So I smile and say, "You're safe now."

"No," she quietly whispers back. "They'll come for me."

"What do you mean?" I ask.

She turns around and faces the wall without responding. The water runs down her back in rivulets, washing away the blood as if it was never there. She rubs her face and looks up at the showerhead, opening her mouth to let it all in. And I just stand there and watch her do it. I'm not just a creeper. Not just a watcher. I'm an admirer.

A worshipper … of her strength and beauty.

Her fearlessness.

And the dangerously intoxicating look hidden in the eyes of a murderer.

I love it all.

"I know you killed her. There's no need to hide it."

"I'm not hiding anything," she replies. "Look." She holds her hands together and forms a pool of water, which quickly turns richly red. "That's Latisha … going down the drain."

"Why did you do it?" I ask, goose bumps scattering across my back.

"She attacked me first."

"Okay, I get that. What happened?"

"I found her cleaning off the blood from her hands after she'd murdered Jordan and attacked Camilla for witnessing the whole thing."

I frown. "How do you know she—"

"Camilla had a cut on her nose and bruises. Latisha carried a knife, and she had bruises too."

I nod, coming to terms with the information.

It makes sense. I've always known Latisha had a crush on my brother. On the video footage, I could see her stalking his room all the time, and in her sleep, she'd call out his name. But that she'd actually commit murder just to win a place beside Anthony surprises me.

"I never actually thought she'd do it," I say.

"What?" Naomi's brows draw together. "You thought …" Her lips part and her face turns dark. "You knew she'd do this."

I cock my head and smile, not wanting to give her any

motivation to hate me. I've already done that enough.

"No." She shakes her head slowly. "You gave her the idea, didn't you?"

I put up my hands. "Hey, now … I'm not that morbid. Although …" I scratch my chin. "She did tell me that she loved him so much, she'd do anything to get him. And I told her that I wasn't going to stand in her way. I guess she took it as a sign of approval."

Slowly but surely, Naomi starts to laugh. And not just softly. Loud. Like she's gone insane.

"This is so … fucking … funny."

"What is?" I ask.

"She was so set on winning that she went and killed all of my opponents, including herself."

My lip quirks up into an awkward smile. "I guess you could say that."

"Ha … so ironic."

She turns off the shower and looks at me. "I'm clean now." I turn, and she walks past me like it's not a big deal, grabbing a towel to wrap herself with.

As I walk after her, someone bangs on my door and jerks the handle. "Open up, Max."

It's Anthony.

Naomi stands up after hearing the sound, and she stares intently at the door.

He slams his fist onto the wood so hard I can see the door move. "Let us in."

"No. This is my room," I say.

"We need to talk," Devon chimes in.

I guess it's two against one now.

Naomi takes a step closer, so she's next to me. "What

do you want?"

"You killed her."

"So? She was attacking me. It was self-defense." She folds her arms.

"You can't keep her in there forever," Devon says.

"I don't care," I say. "We can outlast you." That's a bluff, but I hope he can't see through it.

"Do you want me to bust this door in? Because I will, dammit," Anthony growls, smashing himself against the hard frame.

Right before Anthony can do it again, I push the key into the lock and turn it, opening the door as he drives himself in like a bull, falling over and smashing his head against my floor.

"Fuck!"

"That's what you get for trying to break in," I muse.

"Fuck you," he says, crawling up.

Devon casually strolls inside. "We just wanna talk. That's all."

"Talk. About what?"

He circles Naomi. "About how you're the only bride left."

"She's not on the market," I hiss.

Anthony pats his legs and arms and says, "All the other brides are dead or gone. I say she is."

Devon suddenly grabs her arm. "I say we take her into the game room and toy with her until we know who the clear winner is. You know. The pregnancy stuff and all. We don't have much more time."

"Let go of me." Naomi tries to jerk away, but he won't let her.

When I step in to intervene, my brother blocks my way. "You know the rules, Max."

"Fuck the rules. You know she's mine. We all committed to one girl. Naomi is *mine*."

"She was ... until she killed the remaining option," Devon muses, shrugging. "Now let's start this game, shall we?"

"Fuck you," Naomi says, and she spits in his face.

He wipes it off and smears it on her face. Then he smacks her.

"You don't want to fucking do this," I growl, and I glare at my brothers. "Trust me."

"My bride and baby are dead. His bride is dead. One of us needs to win, and I'm not giving up that easily," Anthony says.

"Even when your lover just died?" I reply.

"Even then ... The rules are the rules," Devon says as if he knows everything.

Fuckers.

"I'm not going to let this go without a fight," he adds. "So let's just get this over with."

I give one look at Naomi and nod.

She immediately rams her elbow into Devon's stomach, causing him to buck and heave and allowing her to escape. She runs out the door, while Anthony looks over his shoulder at the commotion and yells, "Fuck! Come back!"

My brothers race after her, and I follow behind them. Naomi rushes up the stairs in her thin towel that barely covers her body as she tries to escape their grasp. I quickly pick up the gun from the floor and run up the stairs after them. They're already way ahead in the hallways, and I can hear them run in circles up and down the staircases, in and out of rooms with two doors. Our house is like a maze, and I know she realizes this. When she asked if she could explore it, I already knew she was going to memorize every nook and cranny to form a possible escape plan, should she ever need one.

Like now.

When my brothers are hunting her like predators hunt prey.

As I finally manage to catch up to them, Devon reaches for Naomi's foot and pulls her down, making her fall down a few flight of stairs.

"Let her go right now, or I swear to god I will fucking kill you!" I scream at him.

She manages to kick him in the face and clambers back to her feet, running further up to the attic. Anthony shoves me and runs after her, but I won't let myself be caught off guard.

As Devon tries to get up without even looking at me, without even acknowledging the fact that she's mine, I rush toward him and try to cut him off.

I grab him by the collar and pull him back, but he launches his fist in my stomach in response. I cough and heave then return by smashing his head into my knee. We fight and struggle for power, all while Naomi is in trouble. I can't let this continue.

So in a last-ditch effort, I point the gun at him.

He tries to push my arm away, and I shoot multiple times at the wall, bullets ricocheting everywhere. One of them even hits him in the thigh. He howls and grabs his leg, still trying to fend me off.

Too late.

With my gun to his temple, I pull the trigger.

One shot is all it takes to bring him down.

And it doesn't even faze me.

26

MAX

I proceed with my chase, jumping over the steps my brother's body occupies, and I slam open the door to the attic. On the floor lies Naomi's towel, and when I look to my right, Anthony's got her pinned to the wall.

She struggles as he tightly grips her throat, choking her, while he grabs her naked pussy with his other hand.

"You took the opportunity to win this game from me. So now, I'll take what I want from you," he growls.

"Over my dead fucking body," I growl as I walk up to him with my gun pointed straight at his temple. "Die."

Click.

However, the damn gun doesn't fucking go off.

It's fucking empty.

"Fuck."

My brother laughs. Then he releases Naomi from his grasp and grabs my face, smashing me into the wall. I groan in pain as he slams his knee into my stomach and then smacks me into the wall again. But between his massive hits, I manage to turn around and duck and tackle him, making him tumble to the floor.

There, I sit on top of him and punch him repeatedly in the face. However, he quickly overpowers me, rolling over me in an effort to squeeze the fucking life out of me.

"Now, you'll feel what all those other girls have felt," Anthony growls, as he wraps his hands around my throat and starts to choke me.

"Tell me, how does it feel, Max?" he asks with a devious grin on his face.

From the corner of my eye, I spot Naomi grabbing a vase from one of the dusty cabinets, and she runs toward us, smashing the vase on his head.

He falls to the floor, releasing me, and I take the opportunity to get on top of him again. I reach into my pocket and take out the only thing I have. My keys.

And I ram them into his chest as hard as I can.

Again and again.

The terror of his screams goes through marrow and bone as I plunge the cold, hard metal into his heart, and I don't even fucking care. I just want this motherfucker to die.

So I stab him in his neck, stopping him from uttering another word.

Blood sprays out on all sides. I don't know how many times I stab him. Fifteen times, maybe. Enough to create a pool of blood under him.

My hands are covered by the time Naomi says, "You

can stop now." She stands beside me, naked, her feet covered in my brother's blood. Only after hearing her voice do I let go of the bloody keys. The sound of them dropping to the floor is deafening.

I roll off him and let my body drop to the floor. Staring at the ceiling above me, I burst out into stupid laughter. Finally, it's over. I win.

"It's done, Naomi," I whisper. "I killed them."

Naomi leans over me, cocking her head as she gazes at me with a peculiar look in her eyes. A smile spreads on her lips, and she goes to her knees in front of me. She hovers over me, gripping my collar, and whispers, "What now?"

"Now"—I let my finger brush her cheeks, leaving a red stripe in its place—"you become mine for good."

Her smile grows, and she presses her lips to mine. I greedily accept her kiss, even when I'm lying in a pool of my brother's blood.

I can feel it seeping into my hair, dripping down my fingers, but still, I let my hand roam freely across her body. I grab her hair and kiss her deeply, firmly to assert my dominance. I'm the fucking man, and she is the woman I fucking killed for. No one will take her from me, and I will take her now.

My cock grows with the excitement of her beautiful body lying on top of me, and her pretty face smiling back at me after having been through hell. So I kiss her harder and push her against me, squeezing her ass because it and everything else about her belong to me.

Our breaths are hot with arousal, and her hand reaches down between my legs, her fingers around my waistband. She tugs down my sweatpants and pulls my dick out. I'm so hard for her she moans out loud at the feel of me, and when I feel how fucking wet she is for me, I thrust in immediately. She moans out loud as she undulates on top of me, fucking me hard.

Neither of us cares about the two dead bodies, nor do we care that we're covered in blood. And if I'm really honest, it only makes this sickly hot.

She fucks me so hard I feel like I'm a dildo that she's riding, but I love it all the same. She sits up, and I take the opportunity to squeeze her tits and twist her nipples. However, she immediately grabs my wrists and pins them to the floor. The animalistic sounds coming from her mouth, the growling, tell me something. It tells me this isn't just fucking for the release. It isn't just fucking for the pleasure. It's fucking for power.

And the moment she softens her grip, I clutch her arms and roll her over with force. She growls and tries to bite me, but I retaliate with a swift thrust into her pussy. My cock forces her into silence as I stare into her eyes and command her to do my pleasing.

When I smash my lips onto hers, she bites, but I lick up the blood with a smirk. Then I lean up and grab her by the chin, making her look at me as I slam into her. My brother's blood is smudged across her face and tits, and I love how fucking primal it looks. How fucking horny it makes me.

Her hands are trying to grasp me to roll me over again and get her on top, but I'm not letting her get close. Instead, I pin her to the floor and fuck her even harder. She opens her legs even farther and moans when I take her nipple between my teeth and tug.

I know she likes what I do ... but she can't help always

trying to be at the top.

It's what we do.

Who we are.

Fighters. Winners. Conquerors.

And in each other, we've found our match.

Her hand reaches between her legs, and she furiously starts masturbating as I fuck her pussy raw. She's so tight and wet that I lose control, and I close my eyes for just a second to enjoy the sensations.

Only to find me rolling around again and having her end up on top of me. She slams me down on the floor and holds my hand down harder as she swivels around on my cock. She brings her blood-soaked finger to my mouth and makes me suck on it. One of my hands is free, and I use it to flick her clit, making her moan out loud.

A few seconds later, her eyes roll into the back of her head, and I can feel her muscles tighten all around me. Wetness coats my cock, and I come undone.

Howling, I come inside her, my seed pulsing deep into her pussy, just like it should.

She holds my hand in place over her clit, as if to signify that it belongs there. That she's not only mine, but that I'm also hers.

Breathing heavily, she slowly falls down on top of me, my cock still inside her. She rests her head on my chest, and I listen to her breaths as she listens to my heart. I pet her hair, which is still slick from blood and sweat, and I wonder if this is the best sex I've had in my entire life.

"Is it over now?" she mutters suddenly.

I smile as she lifts her head with a curious look on her face. "Yes, it is ... and you won."

27

Accompanying Song: "*Technically, Missing*" *by Trent Reznor &*
Atticus Ross

Naomi

A week later

I hold my mom's hand as I hand her the last envelope.

"Oh, honey ..." she murmurs. "You don't have to do this."

"Open it," I say.

She parts her lips. "But you haven't even told me where you've been yet. How your vacation was."

"Doesn't matter," I say. "Just open it."

She sighs and does what I ask and then her jaw drops when she sees the numbers on the check. "F-fifty million ..." she stutters. "I can't take this."

I squeeze her hand. "I want you to use this money to pay off your debts and Dad's medical bills. And"—I pause to slowly unravel my hand from hers—"this is the last time you'll receive money from me."

"Thank you. I don't know what to say," she says, tears welling up in her eyes.

I cock my head. "Well, you can start by apologizing."

She frowns. "What do you mean?"

I lean back. "I wasn't on vacation, and I think you know this."

She shakes her head, but I place a finger on my lips to silence her.

"I know I'm adopted, but ..." Her eyes widen when I say these words. "I also know you received me from a man in exchange for a deal."

"Nao—"

"Shh," I interrupt. "It's too late to deny it. I know the truth now." I lean in and grasp both her hands, pinning them to the table. "What you did was wrong, and you know that."

She licks her lips and sucks on the bottom one but doesn't respond.

"But you can do the right thing now," I say.

Her face turns dark, and her eyes fill with guilt. "I know what we did, and I always regretted it. We just ... we wanted a baby girl so badly; we'd do anything for it. I didn't know what that man needed you for. Tell me he didn't hurt you," she pleads.

"He didn't. But what's been done can't be undone. You made sure of that."

She swallows. "I'm sorry, Naomi. I really am. And your

dad is too. We can never make it up to you." A tear rolls down her cheek. "But we love you. We really do, with all our heart."

I narrow my eyes. "Prove it to me."

"What do you want me to do? I'll do anything," she mutters.

"Anything?" I ask.

Without hesitation, she says, "Anything."

I smile at that admission. It's precisely what I wanted. Exactly what I needed from her. Her full and utter attention.

And finally … some retribution.

***

A few weeks later

"Honey …" I call out from the bathroom. "How much did your brothers actually own in the company?"

"What, you mean shares? I don't know … same as me, I suppose," he calls back.

"And how much is that?" I ask.

"Pfft … seventeen percent. Maybe Devon's was sixteen. I don't know."

I spit out my toothpaste and look at my teeth in the mirror. They seem even shinier than normal. "What happened to those shares? They must've been transferred to someone else, right? They wouldn't just disappear."

It takes him a while to answer. "No … my father gave them to me because I'm the only one left."

"Interesting. So you own like fifty percent of the

company then?"

"Yes. Father just doesn't like having shares outside the company."

"Hmm …" I reply, not saying much else.

"Why do you want to know?"

"Oh, no reason. Just curious," I muse. Then I grab the home pregnancy testing kit and take out the stick.

I sit on the toilet and pee on the absorbent end, after which I flush and hold it up above the sink, waiting until the results are in. I hum in agreement at the results.

How surprising. *Not.*

The pieces of the puzzle are coming together. It's all falling into place.

I walk out of the bathroom and into our master bedroom, which has now been completely renovated, along with all the other rooms in the mansion. I couldn't stand seeing the same furniture that Devon, Anthony, and the eight other girls had used. It just didn't feel right. So with a smidge of paint, a little bit of retouching, and mostly new chairs, tables, curtains, and beds, all the rooms have been transformed into a beautiful, lavish home. After Max had called the baggers and they had cleaned up all the mess, of course. They even helped him create fake stories about the deaths of all the girls, attributing it to vacation horrors such as bad weather and freak accidents. And for his brothers, of course. They had an unfortunate falling out that resulted in one killing the other then committing suicide with a gun. I wonder what his father will say. I'm not sure which version of the story we'll tell him.

Regardless, we now live without worries, without having to care about their families. *And* we have a special guest room, a gaming room, and even a newly built relaxing spa.

That's what happens when you're the soon-to-be-wife of an heir to a billion-dollar company, which deals with more billions of dollars. You get whatever you ask for. No questions asked.

So now, I stand in the middle of the room in front of our king-size bed, on which Max is comfortably reading a book, and I slowly slide off my robe.

"Oh …" Max raises his eyes above his book. "What's this?"

I smile and turn my body around, touching my stomach. "Do you notice anything?"

His eyes widen, and a wicked smile spreads across his lips. "Are you pregnant?"

I nod.

He throws his book down onto the bed and immediately jumps off and comes toward me. He grabs the back of my head and kisses me straight on the lips. "Congratulations."

"To the both of us," I murmur.

He smiles and kisses me again. "I love you so much …"

It's the first time he's said it to me like that. I don't really know how to respond. "Love you too," I say awkwardly. I'm not sure, but it feels like the first time I'm genuine and honest about my own emotions.

"A baby," he mutters, touching my belly. "Is it really there?"

I show him the stick. "That's what it says."

"Wow." He grins. "Finally."

"So …" I place my hands on his shoulders and push him down. "You know what to do now."

He frowns. "How so?"

I narrow my eyes. "You know what I want."

There's a glimmer in his eyes, and after a few seconds, he drops to one knee and grabs my hand.

"Naomi Lee … will you officially be my bride now?"

"Where's my ring?" I muse.

"I will get you one tomorrow. With diamonds," he adds as if that will make me happier.

I smile, gently squeezing his hand. "All right."

"Is that a yes?"

"Yes. Of course, I will marry you, Max Marino."

He comes up and kisses me on the lips again. "Mrs. Naomi Marino." He grins. "How does it sound?"

"Brilliant," I reply.

"Better get used to it because I'm not letting you go. Not after this news." He places his hand on my belly and smiles. I suppose a way of asserting dominance over something, or someone, that hasn't even been born.

I return the smile, but it's not one of happiness.

It's one of imminent victory.

Mrs. Naomi Lee Marino. The last bride left standing.

28

Accompanying Song: "Technically, Missing" by Trent Reznor & Atticus Ross

Naomi

A few days later

As I leave my own apartment for the last time, my finger travels along the cabinet, and I wipe away the dust that's collected. Such a silly thing, to be attached to a broken place like this. To even remotely feel sad about leaving and never returning. I suppose it's mostly the fact that this is where I first realized what was truly happening in my life. The magnitude of the choices I made in my life and those that others made shaped my very existence.

That ... and the fact that this stack of papers I'm holding in my hand is the only thing I have left of my old life makes me feel like I'm stepping into a whole new one. A whole new me. Like I've transformed and put on a new skin.

If only my past self knew what was coming. I'd have never been sad about my lonely, poor life. Not a single day.

***

As I walk into the living room of the mansion, I see Max sitting on the couch, watching television while looking over some notes his father sent him. I close the doors and check to see if anyone else is here. When the coast is clear, I walk up to him and wrap my arms around him to hug him from behind.

Max Marino, husband of Naomi Lee Marino.

We married on a whim in City Hall. No party. No guests. No fuss. Just the two of us. Well, and that baby growing inside me, of course.

"Hey ..." Max says, kissing my arm as he continues to look over his papers.

"Those are from your father?" It's more of a statement than a question, but I already know. What else could it be?

"Yeah, company things."

"Right." I nod, not really caring. "Did you send all the staff home for today?"

"Not yet. Donna's still up on the second floor, cleaning the bathrooms. Why?"

"Oh ... you know ..." I snigger.

"Well, she told me she's wearing earbuds to listen to some music while she cleans, so ... if you want to do something, nobody will hear."

"Good," I muse, and I step away from him.

I didn't ask because I want to do something. At least not the something he's thinking of. My ideas of *doing something* are entirely different and much more poignant.

I reach into my pocket and take out a knife that I've been carrying around all day, preparing for this moment.

"Turn around," I say, and when he does, he drops his papers and his jaw too.

"What are you doing?" he growls.

The knife is pointed at my belly.

"Claiming my end of the deal," I say without even a sliver of emotion.

"Put that down," he says, holding up his hands like he can do something about it when I'm clearly in control.

"No."

"Listen to me," he says, getting up from the couch. "You don't want to do that."

"I'll do it if you don't shut up," I say. "Now. Sit. Down." I point at the chair beside me, right behind the small table.

He does what I ask, slowly striding toward it, his eyes zoomed in on the knife.

"Don't do anything stupid," I say, clutching the knife.

"Why are you doing this?" he asks. "That's our baby, Naomi. Ours."

"Exactly."

"Why would you want to hurt our baby?" he asks.

"I don't, and I won't," I say.

"If ..." he adds.

Obviously, he knows there's *always* an if.

I pull out the papers from my other pocket and place them on the table in front of him, then I step back to make sure he's out of reach of the knife.

"You signed this. I signed this. This is our contract," he says.

"Exactly … and in it, it states that you will give me fifty percent of your shares and give my parents the other half."

"Bullshit," he growls, slamming his fist on the table. "That part was only viable if you received—"

"Permanent damage." I cock my head and then touch my belly when he still hasn't figured it out.

"A baby," he mutters. "Permanent damage?"

"Oh, Max … didn't you realize? That's what happens to a woman's body when she gets pregnant. It changes. And it never turns back the way it used to be."

His nostrils flare. "You set me up."

As his posture strengthens, I push the knife further into my belly, almost puncturing my skin. "Don't. Move."

"You threaten our baby, put his life and yours at stake … for what?"

"Fifty percent of your shares. And my parents get the other half. That's it."

"You're stripping me of all my shares," he says.

"Think of it as a dowry," I muse, smiling like the crazy motherfucker I am. "Now … If you can grab the paper on the bottom, please."

He does what I ask and pulls it out from under the contract. It's a completely new one. One that relinquishes him of all his shares. "Sign it," I say.

He throws me one last, angry glance before picking up the pen on the table and slowly penning his signature.

"What will you do with it, huh? It's just money. I could give you the world, anything you want. Why are you still unhappy?"

"I just want what I want, Max. Take it or leave it."

Right before he writes the final letter, he says, "What if I say no?"

"Then you lose your child and wife … just like your brother. And when that happens, I doubt you'll be able to save yourself from the same fate he met."

He makes a fist with his free hand, but the other one signs the final letter, finalizing the deal.

"Good. Now grab your phone and call the one who's in charge of the shares. Tell him to give everything to me and show me proof of the transaction." I point at the knife. "Then, and only then, will your baby … and I … be safe."

I wait beside him as he makes the call and finishes the deal. Once he puts down the phone, he says, "It's done." The sound of defeat in his voice makes me sigh. "He sent you a copy of ownership via email."

I nod and slowly back away from him.

However, Max charges toward me, grabs my arm before I can even attempt to strike, and forces me to drop the knife. He shoves me against the wall, my wrists pinned under his strong hands.

"Why?" he says through gritted teeth. "Why did you have to do this?"

"You know why …" I hiss.

"Power? Is that all you want? Will anything ever make you happy enough?"

My lips perk up. "This just might."

His forehead leans against mine in a furious battle of wits. "I just gave away my entire inheritance. My rights to my father's company. All for a baby you wished to kill." He places his hand on my belly and squeezes a little. "I'd rather die with you than let that happen."

I shake my head and smile. "And you honestly think I would kill her," I muse.

He frowns, grinding his teeth, whispering, "It was a bluff?"

I blink a couple of times and look him directly in the eyes. "Do you know me, Max Marino?"

His nostrils flare. "I should've known …"

"Yes, you should've," I say.

"You've been planning this for weeks," he mutters. "The moment you were pregnant, you knew you were going to do this. That's why you asked all those questions about the shares."

"Longer," I say.

"From the beginning?" He narrows his eyes when I nod. He shakes his head. "I can't believe it."

"What? That you've finally met your match?"

He grabs my chin and holds me in place. "That my own wife would set me up."

I smirk. "You said if I married you, I could have anything I wanted. This is what I wanted."

He plants his hands beside me on the wall, trapping me between his arms. "The company?"

"Power …" I murmur, seductively looking up into his eyes. "Sweet … delicious … power."

"Power. Nothing beats the feeling of having it, and you just took it all away from me," he whispers, inching closer.

"I am still your wife, Max," I say with a hushed voice. "My shares are your shares."

"But you just wanted them to be in your hands, not

mine."

"Exactly," I muse, glancing at him as his lips draw closer.

"Fuck me," he murmurs, his lips hovering so close to mine I can almost taste them. "You're one crazy woman."

"And you're in love with her," I muse. "So what does that make you?"

"Insane." He licks his lips, and then he kisses me, nibbling my lip until he draws blood. The taste enters my mouth, and I laugh, kissing him back. I know he'll never leave me. He can't. I owned his heart, and now, I own his empire too.

"You're a fucking vixen," he growls, his hands disappearing under my shirt. "But you rile me up so much that it makes me want to fuck you."

"Do it." I hiss. "Fuck me. Show me how much I'm yours."

His hands roam freely across my breasts, and when he finds my nipples, he twists them until I squeal.

"You want to be punished so badly?" he muses. "C'mon then." He suddenly spins me around, pulls down my yoga pants, and tears down his zipper. "I'll show you how insane I can get."

I know what's coming next … and I love every fucking second of it.

EPILOGUE

Accompanying Song: "Take A Bow" by Muse

A month later

I look at the letter my mom sent me and smile before crumpling it up and throwing it into the fire. I take the item she sent me from the envelope and tuck it into my pocket before Max can see it. Then I grab the paper lying on the coffee table in front of me and read over it again, gloating over the fact that it mentions my name under Marino's company.

"Are you coming?"

I turn my head to see Max walking toward me.

"Of course," I reply, tucking the paper into the pocket of my coat.

Like I could ever forget where we're going today. For the first time ever, I'm meeting his father. Finally.

I get up from the seat and button my coat. Walking past the pool table, I briefly touch the green fabric and smile to myself as I realize that it's all mine now.

"Let's go," Max says as he escorts me out the door.

The drive feels agonizingly slow and long, but in my heart, I know it's worth every damn second. With my hand resting on my belly, I tell my little one in my head that he will be one of the most powerful kids in the world.

"Your father," I say as I turn my head toward Max. "Do you two get along?"

He makes a face. "Is this a serious question?"

"Dead serious." I frown. "Be honest."

"I hate his fucking guts," he says, which makes me chuckle. "But he is my father," he adds.

"Why do you hate him so much?"

"I think that should be clear by now … shouldn't it?" he says with a smirk on his face.

"Right." I nod, and then I stare out the window again.

Funnily enough, when we're finally at our destination, it's the building opposite of where I first met Max.

I squint at him, and he laughs like he knows exactly what I'm thinking as he gets out of the car and walks to my side to let me out like the chivalrous man he is. I take his hand, and he takes me inside, into an almost identical company building—only this one is much, much larger. Enormous even, and there are so many floors to gaze up at, so many people bustling around, that it's impossible to guess how many work here. I guess you don't get billions of dollars out of nowhere.

"Good day, sir." A man greets us. He escorts us to the gold-colored elevator with red carpeting and lets us inside, pressing the button for us. The luxury of it all feels so good as we go up and up ... and up. It never seems to come to a stop.

Minutes pass before the doors finally open, and the man nods at us to step out. "Thank you," Max says.

"My pleasure," the man replies, and he goes back down with the elevator again, leaving us alone.

Again, only one door is at the end of the hallway. I take a deep breath and start walking. With Max by my side, I feel confident, but with this baby inside me, I feel invincible.

With my head held high, I stride toward the door, and I don't even knock before entering.

In a room, at the end of a long table, sits a fat man with a white, scruffy beard, smoking a thick cigar.

He looks up from underneath his small glasses and sets down the documents he was reading. "How nice of you to knock." He puts his cigar down, and the little red box carrying more of them draws my attention.

I smile wickedly. "How nice of you to finally invite your daughter-in-law for a first time meet-up."

He raises one brow and stares at Max, who just shrugs, not caring about any of it.

"Well, I must say, I never expected this one to win," he mutters, clearing his throat. "Out of all the girls you could've picked—"

"We've been through this already, Father. I don't want your opinion," Max interrupts.

"So you're the girl he wants, huh?" His father changes positions in his black leather chair and leans back on the armrest, inspecting me as if he has a say in it. "Welcome to the family." His voice is deep and ugly, just like his face.

"Thanks," I sneer.

"Not very grateful, is she?" his father says to Max, completely ignoring my presence.

"Excuse me?" I say, folding my arms. "You haven't even introduced yourself yet. My name is Naomi Lee Marino."

His father frowns and glares at Max for a brief amount of time. "Already married, huh?"

"Father," Max growls.

He holds up his hand. "Don't worry. I get it. I've been young too once." Now he directs his attention toward me. "Nolan Marino. Such a pleasure to meet you, *daughter-in-law.*" The last words come out in a condescending tone.

"Now ... Max, let's get to the real reason why you're here, shall we?" he says, scooting his chair back to stand up. He places his hands on the long table. "Tell me what happened to them."

"They all either died or left."

"I'm not talking about the girls." He waves his hand. "I couldn't care less what happened to them."

Their whole existence waved away ... just like that.

"How could you say that? You just threw their lives away like it was nothing," I growl.

"I wasn't the one who killed them or let them go," he says sourly. "Not that that's important. Only one was supposed to be left, and that's exactly what happened."

"You intended for all of them to go away? What about the fifty million dollars promised to them?"

"Oh, honey ... you didn't think I'd actually pay fifty

million to all of the girls?" He chuckles. "I would've killed them myself if push came to shove."

I look at Max. "You said we'd still get the money."

"They didn't stay for the entire three weeks, did they?" His father's lips quirk up into a devilish smile. "So the contract doesn't even stand."

Grinding my teeth, I think of how smart I was for including a clause to safeguard my fifty million.

The man purses his fat lips. "Now ... tell me what happened to your brothers."

"We killed them," I say.

Both of their eyes are on me now, and I can see the rage in his eyes bubbling up to the surface. It feels like getting a shot of heroine ... so fucking good.

"They almost killed us first," Max adds, to soften the blow.

His father's hand balls into a fist. "Why?"

He already knew they were dead. We had already told him, but he never responded to our letter.

"Because all the other girls had died and only she was left. They wanted her, but she was already mine."

He flops back down in his chair and sighs, rubbing his forehead. "So you just decided to kill them?"

"It was either them or us," Max says. "And I don't regret it. Not even for one second."

"So you won," his father mutters, and then he slowly bursts out into laughter. "That is just amazing."

Max and I give each other strange looks. Now I understand where all the insanity in the brothers came from. His father is even worse.

"You won, against all odds." His father points at Max as

if it's some sort of surprise. "I put my bets on Anthony, but you played the game so well. God ..." He grins and bites his knuckles.

"You're not even a little upset that your sons died?" I ask.

"I knew it was coming," he says, with a shrug. "It's the only way the game can end."

I suck in a breath. "Only one can win ... so that's what that means."

"What else could it mean? Do you think I'd let all of them fuckers run my company? No, they'd make a mess." He slams his hand on the table. "My grandfather had to bend over backward in order to save this company from the bankruptcy caused by his negligent brothers. Do you think it was easy for him? No, but he did what he had to do, and he knew there was no way for three men to be the head of an empire without ruining it, so he killed them. And then he taught my father, and he did the same, and so it goes on and on."

His rant makes me suck in a breath.

"Don't act so goddamn uptight, like you don't know what kind of power we're dealing with here," he growls. "This company is too great to fall. There's a reason a country only has one king. This is no different. This company needs a strong hand to rule. One. Not three."

"Have you always been this insane?" I blatantly ask.

He looks at me as if I'm joking and then proceeds to laugh. "Of course not. My father did this with my brothers and me, and now, I did it with all of you. It's how things work in this company."

I look at Max, who says, "It's true. My uncles have been

292

dead for a long time."

"Too bad my wife died too." His father leans back in his chair with his arms folded behind his head. "Although maybe that's because I was a bit rough on her."

I ball my fists, my nails digging into my hand. "You're a monster."

"Why? Because I only want what's best? Because I give only the winner what he deserves?" He slams his fist down on the table again. "Let me tell you this, lady. You have no fucking clue what it takes to run a company this huge. This powerful. It takes more than just handling money. It takes cunning skill. It takes a smart mind."

He taps his fingers on the table. "And ... it takes a ruthless person. Someone who isn't afraid to weed out the unnecessary and deal with it."

"You mean someone like you," I growl. "Someone who killed parents to get their children, giving them to strangers and bribing them to keep quiet."

His eyes narrow once I say those words.

"Yeah, that's right. I know. I know every dirty little lie you've told, every filthy thing you've done."

"Oh, yes ... I did what was necessary to get the right girls for my boys. And you ... are perfect." As he stares at my naked legs underneath my skirt, he grins like he already owns me. *Motherfucker.*

"But all that doesn't matter," he says with a voice that makes my skin crawl. "You belong to our family now, and now that the game is finally over, you can settle. Have a family. I read in the letter that you were pregnant. Congratulations. Exactly as we want." His father smiles gleefully. "You can happily grow old together, have more kids, and when the time comes, they can start the game again and decide who becomes the next heir to the company. But for now, let's get to business. After all, with his brothers gone, Max now owns half the company, and when I die, it will all go to him."

For the first time since I came here, I smile, and I walk toward the man, pull the paper from my pocket, and slam it on the table. "Wrong." I point at the name at the top. "See this? I am the owner of your company now."

I point at the numbers, each individual share of the brothers, which now belong to me, along with the one percent my parents owned for keeping quiet about me … That percentage of shares they couldn't even touch until I was married to one of the brothers … The exact same shares of which the ownership was transferred to me as a final request from me for all the years they lied to my face.

The man laughs and scoffs, "Ridiculous …" But he stops talking the moment he reads it. "Wha—"

"I hold all the power … and this game ends now." With my other hand, I pull the gun I'd been concealing this entire time and shoot him in the head, point-blank.

His face drops to the table, smudging the paper with his blood as I grin wickedly.

Behind me, I can hear Max suck the air into his lungs as he clutches the table. "You killed him …" His voice falters a little.

"I guess there's one thing your cameras can't do … and that's looking inside my head," I muse. I've wanted to do this for so long. I turn to face him and say, "Are you angry?"

He swallows, pausing to take a few breaths; the look in his eyes is uncertain but relieved. "No. But … *fuck*."

"You know why he had to go." I clean the gun with my shirt, meticulously brushing all the nooks and crannies.

"Because he put you in the game," Max says.

"You didn't think I'd just take the fifty million dollars and be happy with it, did you?" I muse.

"How do you plan to get away with this?" he asks.

"Simple." I shove the fat body off the chair, and it drops to the floor like a sack of potatoes. "We make it look like a suicide."

Max rubs his forehead, staring at the scene in front of him. "Jesus Christ."

"Take a picture. Get your baggers to clean him up. Write it off as a man gone crazy due to losing his sons. Easy." I smile and shrug. Then I place the gun in his father's hand and put his finger on the trigger.

"So what now?" he mutters.

I cock my head. "What now? Well ... we're still husband and wife, and we have a baby coming soon."

Max shakes his head slowly. "Are you going to kill me too now that you've got the company under your thumb?"

He never takes his eyes off me as I grab the black leather chair, pull it back, and sit down on it. I stare him down and say with a sultry voice, "I won't kill you. You can be with me now." I grab a cigar from the red box and light one up. One tiny whiff won't hurt.

With a devious grin on my face, I add, "But ... only under *my* terms. My rule."

Then I spread my legs, exposing my naked pussy.

I always liked going commando.

Cocking my head, I watch Max gravitate toward me and drop to his knees.

As he buries his face between my legs, I close my eyes and let my head drop back, enjoying the taste of victory. He knows what's needed, what's required, and with his future resting in my lap, there's only one thing he can do.

Submit.

THANK YOU
FOR READING!

Thank you so much for reading Wicked Bride Games. I hope you enjoyed the story!

For updates about upcoming books, please visit my website, www.clarissawild.blogspot.com or sign up for my newsletter here: www.bit.ly/clarissanewsletter.

I'd love to talk to you! You can find me on Facebook: www.facebook.com/ClarissaWildAuthor, make sure to click LIKE. You can also join the Fan Club: www.facebook.com/groups/FanClubClarissaWild/ and talk with other readers!

Enjoyed this book? You could really help out by leaving a review on Amazon and Goodreads. Thank you!

ALSO BY CLARISSA WILD

Dark Romance
Delirious Series
Killer & Stalker
Mr. X
Twenty-One
Ultimate Sin
VIKTOR

New Adult Romance
Fierce Series
Blissful Series
Ruin

Erotic Romance
The Billionaire's Bet Series
Enflamed Series
Bad Teacher

Visit Clarissa Wild's website for current titles.
http://clarissawild.blogspot.com

ABOUT THE AUTHOR

Clarissa Wild is a New York Times & USA Today Bestselling author, best known for the dark Romance novel Mr. X. Her novels include the Fierce Series, the Delirious Series, Stalker, Twenty-One (21), Ultimate Sin, Viktor, Bad Teacher, and RUIN. She is also a writer of erotic romance such as the Blissful Series, The Billionaire's Bet series, and the Enflamed Series. She is an avid reader and writer of sexy stories about hot men and feisty women. Her other loves include her furry cat friend and learning about different cultures. In her free time she enjoys watching all sorts of movies, reading tons of books and cooking her favorite meals.

Want to be informed of new releases and special offers? Sign up for Clarissa Wild's newsletter on her website clarissawild.blogspot.com.

Visit Clarissa Wild on Amazon for current titles.

Printed in Great Britain
by Amazon